DO NO HARM

Also by Danielle Singleton

Safe & Sound

Connect with the author online:

www.daniellesingleton.com
@auntdanwrites
www.facebook.com/singletondanielle

Do No Harm

Danielle Singleton

This book is a work of fiction and any resemblance to persons, living or dead, or places, events, or locales is purely coincidental. The characters are productions of the author's imagination and used fictitiously.

ISBN: 1482744317

******

To Mom and Dad:
For Everything

"Honor your father and your mother, that your days may be long in the land that the Lord your God is giving you."
Exodus 20:12

ACKNOWLEDGMENTS

First on my list of acknowledgments is and will always be my Lord and Savior Jesus Christ.

Thank you to Stacy Clark, who probably never imagined that bringing her healthcare law textbook on spring break would lead to the idea for this story.

A huge thanks once again to my Reading Committee. I don't know what I would do without y'all. Especially to you, Mom, for being my sounding board for this book and Joseph's "cray cray" antics. I'm sorry for spoiling all of the surprises for you!

My sincerest love and appreciation for my two Pops – the late Bernard Blankenship and J. Paul Singleton – two of the best men I've ever known.

Thank you to "Big Josh" Regan for your amazing artwork for the cover. I also want to acknowledge Chris Petersen for his help with the more technical, medical side of things. This author who always took "science for non-science majors" greatly appreciates you helping me sound like I knew what I was talking about!

And thank you again to my big puppy Gus . . . out of all of the paper that you like to steal and eat, you somehow know not to take the pages of my book drafts. Gracias mijo.

I hope y'all enjoy the story.

Do No Harm

****

"I will prescribe regimens for the good of my patients according to my ability and my judgment, and never do harm to anyone."

Oath of Hippocrates of Kos, 5th Century BC

PART I: JOSEPH

ONE

Joseph was fuming. Absolutely livid as he paced around the hardwood floors of his kitchen in his standard everyday attire of khaki slacks and a button-down shirt. "I should've won that award," the doctor hissed to no one in particular. The kitchen was empty except for him, as was the rest of the house. Joseph lived alone. He preferred it that way. Having someone else always underfoot was messy. Inconvenient. And, more than anything else, it got in the way of his research. "Research that deserved to win!"

The slender, well-dressed man in his mid-forties was yelling now, but he was angry enough to yell. All of his hard work, five years spent in his research lab working on a cure for malaria, and he had nothing to show for it. Sure, Joseph had created an excellent prototype for a vaccine and recently sold it to a large pharmaceutical company for several million dollars. But Joseph didn't care about the money. He wanted the fame. The respect. He wanted to be known not only in the science community but also the general public as the best infectious disease researcher alive. Joseph was the best. He knew he was the best. Now the rest of the world needed to know it too.

When he finished pacing, the bachelor doctor walked over to the island in the middle of his kitchen and pressed a security code into the keypad located just underneath the granite countertop. Seconds later, a hiss-pop sound let Joseph know that the secret door was unlocked. Swinging open what to an untrained eye was just the end of the kitchen's island, Joseph ducked his buzz cut, salt-and-pepper colored head and slowly descended the now visible stairs into his private research lab. Originally built as a safe room for his house, Joseph had long ago decided to use the bunker for the research projects that he didn't want anyone to know about. Financed by the money he made from selling drug prototypes to big pharmaceutical companies, Joseph had another small workspace set up on the second floor of his suburban home that other people were allowed to see, on the off chance he happened to have visitors. But this lab was special. This was Joseph's sanctuary. This was where he was working on the project that would force people to recognize just how brilliant he truly was.

It wasn't a new idea, really – the one that Joseph had to make a virus that could kill people. Doctors and researchers put together new viruses all the time. They called them recombinant viruses. Gene therapy techniques were based on the idea. All that was required was a vector (the viral capsid or shell) and the right arrangement of DNA or RNA. That combination of genes would then create proteins to fight against a patient's disease. When done correctly, miraculous things could happen, like new treatments for skin cancer, Parkinson's disease, and leukemia.

Or, as Joseph predicted, very dangerous things could happen. It was his plan to take the tried and true method of gene therapy to engineer a virus that would express a deadly protein. The virus would then be delivered to the body through blood transfusions, although Joseph was still figuring out the best way to get access to that much human blood and deliver it to hospitals. This entire project was a big challenge for him . . . the man who had spent the past several decades of his life focused only on helping patients and curing diseases now had to plot and plan and scheme for not only how to make a new, deadly virus but also how to avoid police detection in the process. It was thrilling, this new adventure of his.

As Joseph sat in his secret underground lab, working to find the right combination of vectors and genes to express the exact deadly protein that he wanted, he couldn't help but get excited about what was to come. Operation Respect, as he had labeled the enterprise, would take a lot of time and effort. Years, perhaps. *But it will also be fun*, he thought with excitement. *Exhausting, a little terrifying probably, but also really, really fun.*

****

A full year and a half passed without Joseph making any significant progress on his secret virus. A lesser man, a lesser doctor, might have gotten frustrated and given up. But Joseph had learned from a very young age how to be patient. His parents, a trauma surgeon and a socialite, hadn't been at all interested in raising their only child. Joseph was convinced that he was only born to satisfy his grandparents' desire for an heir. So he learned to be patient while waiting for his parents to notice him. Or his nannies to feed him. Or a teacher to walk by and let him out of the locker that he was inevitably shoved into at school. Yes, Joseph was a patient man.

Nevertheless, the scheming doctor hadn't anticipated how hard it would be to make the new proteins do exactly what he wanted them to do . . . every time Joseph thought he was close to having it figured out, something would go wrong. The virus would kill too slowly, or wouldn't kill at all. Several prototypes killed like Joseph wanted but would have been way too easy for hospitals to detect and treat.

Part of the problem was inherent in the complicated virus-making process itself, but a large portion of Joseph's troubles were self-imposed. Because he couldn't just make a killer virus and be done with it. If that was the case, Joseph would have been finished with this research stage of Operation Respect several months ago. No, Joseph's virus needed to be more than just a killer. It needed to be a silent killer. Untraceable. Indeed, the image that always came to his mind while working late at night in his safe room-turned-lab was that of military fighter jets. Those highly complex, high-functioning airplanes were endowed with stealth capabilities to keep them from being detected on enemy radar. Joseph, for his part, was creating a stealth virus.

"And both my virus and those flashy airplanes will work in the service of our country, won't they?"

Joseph posed his question to a cage full of little white mice that he was using to test his new viral concoctions. In Joseph's brilliant yet warped mind, what he was doing – designing a virus that would kill, at minimum, dozens of people – was actually a favor to the United States. The victims of his plan, the ones who would die, were unfortunately just the collateral damage in his creative destruction. "America needs to know how great I am," the doctor continued confidently. "They need to understand the groundbreaking quality of research of which I am capable. They don't understand it right now. But they will. And we'll all be better off once they do."

****

"It's ready," Joseph declared as he inspected the results of his latest test run, nearly two years after he first decided to teach the world a thing or two about respecting him and his medical abilities. "It's finally ready." Trial after trial had come up short of what Joseph wanted to create, but now he had finally managed to find the correct combination of vector, gene, and protein. Joseph knew that if this was a professional lab and the project was a new drug, it would need to undergo human trials first before being declared 'ready.' But he was working in different circumstances, and mice testing would simply have to do. Joseph had told the guy at the store that he had a pet snake – how else can you explain needing to buy mass quantities of little white mice? He always paid in cash, too. He couldn't afford to leave any kind of trail.

"Yes, we're ready," Joseph said again, talking as if the deadly virus sitting in vials on the table in front of him was another person, a partner in crime. It was much more fun that way. Instead of a weapon, he had a partner. An assistant in Joseph's bid to finally gain the respect he deserved. No one ever respected him. Not his surgeon father, who thought that doctors who don't cut aren't real doctors at all. Not his mother, who was so in awe of his father that Joseph was merely an afterthought. She skipped her son's medical school graduation to sit in the gallery and watch yet another of Joseph Sr.'s surgeries. No respect. Not the kids at school growing up who always picked on the skinny kid with glasses. No respect. But that would all change soon.

Now I just need the blood, Joseph thought as he stood up from his swivel stool and walked across his secret lab to the small refrigerator in the corner. Opening the door, Joseph inspected the plastic pouches of his own blood that were stored inside. He had donated two pints of his blood to the cause yesterday. Since Joseph was O-negative, or a universal donor, his blood was perfect. It was almost guaranteed to be used.

"But we need more donors, don't we?" Joseph said as he shut the refrigerator door, walked back over to his work station, and lightly stroked the virus vials reverently. "Not a problem, of course, as long as we do it right. It shouldn't be too difficult to find some vagrants who nobody will miss. And then we'll be doing the public yet another favor, won't we? Yes we will," Joseph purred to the deadly concoction on the table in front of him. "A few fewer eye sores on the streets."

The scheming doctor shook his face and shoulders to clear his mind of the thought of dirty, homeless menaces to society. Joseph had absolutely no sympathy for anyone less fortunate than him. "Just natural selection carrying out its work," he declared as he put the vials containing his virus back in the specialized silver cylinder that kept them fresh and clear of any contamination. Joseph then climbed back up the stairs and entered the code that he needed to exit his secret lair. There was a different code for entering and exiting – just in case someone did manage to find out about the room and get down into it, the homeowner wanted to make sure that they never got to leave.

"Time to find myself some blood," he announced.

TWO

"You're not finished yet," Joseph ordered a day later as he stood over the hole that the man in front of him was digging. Joseph didn't know his name, his age, or his life story. Even if he had, he wouldn't have cared. The man wasn't going to be alive much longer anyway.

"I said keep digging!"

Joseph needed to make sure the hole was deep enough that no one would ever find the body. *No body, no murder – right?* he thought. *Never leave a trail.*

The unfortunate victim in the latest part of Joseph's scheme tried to issue a response, but the duct tape over his mouth prevented the escape of any noise. And the fully loaded 9mm Beretta pistol in Joseph's hand prevented any other kinds of escape.

"Alright, that's enough," the man with the gun concluded. "Climb out of there."

It was visibly a struggle for the malnourished homeless man to pull himself out of the approximately four foot deep hole that he had spent the past two hours digging. When he finally rose to his feet on the dirt floor of the national park, a gleam entered Joseph's eyes. The doctor-turned-kidnapper and murderer knew that it was time.

"I couldn't help but notice," Joseph began, "that the hat you're wearing says Iraq War Veteran on it. Are you really a vet or did you just steal the hat?"

The captive nodded his head up and down and pointed to his chest to signal in the affirmative that he had been a soldier.

"Well, thank you for your service," Joseph continued as he took a black silencer out of what would become his blood box and screwed it onto the Beretta. In addition to spending the past year and a half creating his virus, Joseph had also taken the time to file all of the paperwork and get all of the necessary approval to buy a sound suppressor, commonly known as a silencer. He didn't want to run the risk of someone hearing the gunshot. "And now," Joseph continued, "you get to once again be of service to this great country. What do you call it? The ultimate sacrifice?" The doctor grinned. "Because America needs me. They just don't know it yet. And for them to know it, I need your blood."

A tear trickled down the cheek of the thirty-one year old Army veteran as he finally came to terms with what was about to happen. *I did three tours in Iraq and one in Afghanistan and never got a scratch. Only to come back to where it's supposedly safe and be murdered by this psychopath.* The man standing before Joseph slowly closed his eyes and took a deep breath to prepare himself for what came next.

"Sometimes you have to break a few eggs to make an omelet, no?" Joseph said gleefully as he smiled, took the safety off, raised the gun in his right hand, and pulled the trigger.

****

Draining blood from a dead body isn't as easy as one might think. Once the heart stops beating, blood stops flowing through the person's veins. The drip-drip-drip process of a typical blood donation would normally take hours on a dead person. But Joseph didn't have hours. He needed to get the blood from his involuntary donor – a process called exsanguination – as quickly as possible so that he could leave the national park before anyone noticed him. He had tried to come up with a fancy, high-tech way of draining his victims' blood; Joseph had even experimented with a blood sucking machine that resembled the space saver vacuums that are sold on infomercials. But he could never figure out a way to get the blood without bursting all of the blood vessels and veins, so his blood sucking machine idea had to be scrapped.

"And so I'm left with this - the quick and dirty version," Joseph said aloud. He had already inserted needles into twelve different veins on the military veteran's body, and was now attaching tubes and empty blood bags to those needles. The doctor then tossed the empty blood bags into the fresh dirt of the grave that his victim just finished digging and slowly pushed the body over the edge of the hole, sitting on top of the corpse so it wouldn't fall completely over the precipice. With his victim suspended upside-down, gravity worked its magic and the blood bags were full in relatively short order.

"Thank you very much for your generous donation to today's blood drive," Joseph said as he pulled the twelfth and final one pint sized medical blood bag back up from the hole and carefully placed the blood in the climate controlled box beside him. "It will be very helpful with our project."

Joseph then rolled his victim over the edge and watched the body plop down into the large pit in the ground. Picking up the shovel, Joseph filled in the rest of the hole with the same dirt that the homeless veteran had spent the last hours of his life digging out. The man renowned for his life-saving medical research stomped on the fresh earth to flatten it down and then pushed the blood container back and forth a couple of times for good measure, placing sticks and leaves over the spot as a final camouflage.

"Let's go home, my sweets," Joseph purred to the bags of blood in the box at his feet. "I have a wonderful virus that I want to introduce you to."

THREE

Ever since his bullet hit the homeless man's brain and Joseph saw his first victim crumble to the ground, something had been bothering him. It was still bothering him as he sat on the couch in his living room later that night and tried to unwind from the day's events. But no matter how hard he tried, the questions still remained.

What if that guy was a drug addict? Or sick? Or anything that might cause his blood to be rejected by the Red Cross when the donation gets tested at the regional blood bank? Joseph groaned aloud. Did I just kill him for nothing?

Joseph was concerned about waste. But not of some homeless loser's life. He was concerned about wasting his own valuable time. And his even more valuable virus. Joseph had only made a limited amount of the virus, and it would probably spoil if not used in a fairly quick amount of time. Which meant that if the first blood donor turned out to be defective, it would be that much longer until Joseph could create more of his virus and find a blood replacement. A non-defective replacement.

"Shit," Joseph said aloud. "I really should've thought this through more."

****

Despite his concerns about the viability of homeless people's blood, the very next day Joseph found himself out roaming the city once again.

"Excuse me, sir," Joseph called out from his car window, trying to attract the attention of his next blood donor, "I was wondering if you could give me directions to the local homeless shelter? I'm supposed to be volunteering there but can't seem to find the place."

Willie 'Shoes' McRae took one look at the nerdy white dude driving the $60,000 silver sedan and shook his head. *All these rich white folk comin' down here to 'volunteer' and 'help' the poor black folk. When all they really doin' is tryna not feel so guilty 'bout all they money.*

Shoes – people called him that because his street business generally dealt in shoes and socks – turned to face the car and put on what he called his Uncle Tom smile. "Why yessa I can. I was jus' goin' that way mysef."

"Wonderful!" Joseph replied a little too eagerly, before reminding himself to play it cool. "If you're already going there, why don't I just give you a ride?"

Shoes wasn't expecting that response. Rich people, especially rich white people, were always afraid of him. What remained of his graying hair was long and ratty, and he only bathed about once a week, usually when he started to smell so bad that he was willing to walk the four miles round-trip to the men's shelter that had showers. His clothes were all second-, third-, or fourth-hand rags, and since Willie had only gone to the dentist once in his forty-four years (when the city held a free dental clinic about ten years ago), what was left of his teeth were yellowed and rotting. He looked like something straight out of central casting for a dirty vagabond. But this guy, Mr. Silver Sedan, didn't seem afraid of Shoes at all.

Either he be crazy for lettin' me in the car wif him, or I be crazy for gettin' in the car wif him, Shoes thought as he shook his head yet again. "Yessa, that be jus' fine. Thank you sa."

Joseph waited until he drove around the corner and out of sight of his passenger's neighbors under the inner-city bridge before he put his plan into motion.

Step one: lock the doors. The man beside him jumped a little at the 'click' sound of the lock but he didn't say anything. Shoes just looked like he was waiting for the next spot to give directions toward the shelter.

Step two: the gun. This had to be done just right, or else his passenger might start to get ideas about fighting for control of either the pistol or the steering wheel. When Joseph's car came to a stop at a red light, he carefully pushed the button on the car's middle console that made two little doors flip open. Then, in one swift motion, Joseph grabbed the gun from inside the middle compartment and held it flush to his passenger's chest, pointing straight at the other man's heart.

"What the fuck man?" Joseph's latest victim cried out, terror filling his eyes.

The car's driver kept a firm grip on the gun with one hand and the steering wheel with the other as he maneuvered his vehicle through city traffic and on to the interstate, headed in the direction of the nearby Blue Mountain National Park. "Just shut up and be still," he commanded.

Now wasn't the time for talking. Or explaining. His passenger would get an explanation, just like the Army veteran had, but not yet. Right now Joseph needed to focus. There were too many cars around with too many potential witnesses inside them.

****

Thirty minutes later, Joseph and Shoes pulled to a stop in an otherwise-empty parking lot in the middle of Blue Mountain National Park. On the weekends, most of the other parking lots would be full of cars as people came to run the trails. But there weren't any trails in this area of the park. And it was 3:00pm on a Tuesday . . . not exactly prime national park time. Which made it the perfect time for Joseph. He had initially thought he should collect his blood donations at night so it would be dark and he wouldn't have to miss any work, but if a park ranger happened to spot his car at 2:00am he would be screwed.

So Joseph told his office assistant that he would be working in his home lab today to keep her from being suspicious of his absence. And in the middle of the day, if anybody asked what he was doing in the park, Joseph could easily claim he had just been out hiking.

Joseph put his car in park and turned it off. He then reached with his left hand down into the compartment on the inside of his door, pulling out a large role of duct tape. "Give me your hands," he ordered.

"Hell no, homie," Shoes shot back. "Ain't no way you gon' tie me up wif that shit. Nuh-uh. No way," Shoes declared.

"Give. me. your. hands," Joseph repeated, this time digging the gun into his passenger's ribs.

"Okay, okay, fine," Shoes squeaked in response as fear caused his voice to rise several octaves. Returning close to his normal baritone, he added: "but you better not be no gay rapist. I don't go like that man. No. I. don't."

"Would you please just shut up?" his captor growled, quickly losing his patience as he tied the victim's hands together. "Here, let me help you with that," Joseph added as he tore off a piece of duct tape and stuck it over Shoes' mouth. Joseph grinned. "Much better."

The mad scientist then opened his car door and got out, looking around to make sure no one was watching him. He walked to the back of the car, opened the trunk, and pulled out a large box to hold the pouches of blood and the same shovel that his first victim had used. With his gun pointed at today's blood donor, Joseph then began to march them both towards the spot where Shoes would dig his final resting place.

FOUR

The day after he buried Shoes, Joseph was tired. Very tired. He had been researching and planning his virus project for nearly two years, but he never accounted for the fact that actually executing everything would be so physically exhausting. He had to work a full day in his lab or with patients, then rush home to complete the final preparations on Operation Respect during the nighttime hours when he knew he wouldn't be disturbed.

Well, when he was less likely to be disturbed. There was one pesky little girl in the neighborhood who had decided that Joseph must be lonely and taken it upon herself to rectify that situation. She reminded Joseph of little Cindy Lou Who from 'How the Grinch Stole Christmas.' It was actually a fairly apt metaphor, since people who knew Joseph or worked with him might say that he too had a heart that was several sizes too small. *Except my heart is perfectly sized. And I don't want or need a little girl for a friend or an invitation to Christmas dinner.*

Joseph didn't like people; they annoyed him. He just wanted their respect. Deserved their respect. And would have their respect when this project was over. It takes a genius to create a virus like his from scratch – one that can imitate other illnesses, not show up on any existing screening tests, and kill within weeks of exposure. A genius. And Joseph had done it.

But the doctor who neighbors described as "quiet" and "keeps to himself" wasn't in genius mode right now. He was in actor mode. Because right now it was time to convince the third and final blood donor to get in the car with him. It would be harder this time, for sure. After two disappearances in two days, city police had issued an alert warning the homeless population to watch out for a guy driving a light-colored sedan.

Which was why Joseph was now headed east on the interstate to another city nearby where – hopefully – the vagrants there hadn't been warned. "I don't know why the police even bother," Joseph muttered as he fiddled with the radio dial, trying to find a good station. "They're just dirty, no good homeless people. Leeches on society's resources." He shook his head in disgust. "But nooooo, 'every life is precious'," Joseph sneered, imitating the annoying, church-going, life-loving busybodies who unfortunately made up the majority of the volunteers at the hospital where he had privileges.

"Every life is *not* precious," the scientist declared to his windshield. "But every life does have value," he continued, on a roll now. "Take my three vagrants. Seventy-two hours ago they were a drain on the city's resources and scared children at red lights by panhandling. But now, their blood will be used to carry my virus to dozens of people. And then I can expose how vulnerable America's blood supply is, and people will see the kind of work and dedication it took for me to create such a beautiful illness." In Joseph's mind, at that moment, the person he was on his way to murder wasn't actually a person at all. He (or she) was a means to an end at best and collateral damage at worst. The same for the people who would be infected and almost certainly die from his virus. "People die every day. Everybody eventually dies. I'm just moving up their expiration dates a little bit."

Joseph stopped his monologue for a minute as one of his favorite songs came on the radio, appropriately 'Boulevard of Broken Dreams' by Green Day. When the song ended, Joseph concluded: "I'll win the Nobel Prize in Medicine, I'll be famous, and there won't be a single person in the world who will doubt that I am the greatest pathologist who ever lived."

Joseph was smiling now, his vision of the future reenergizing him as he pulled off the interstate and made his way toward the sketchy part of town.

"Yes, my homeless people certainly have value. They're worth twelve pints of blood each." And then, with a chuckle, Joseph added: "alright donor number three, where are you?"

****

Too easy, Joseph thought as he drove past a street corner populated by prostitutes. *One would certainly get in the car with me, but then there's no telling what all of the diseases she undoubtedly picked up on the streets would do to the virus. Plus I could accidentally proposition an undercover cop and get arrested.* Joseph grimaced. "That would certainly mess with my plans," he said. "Plus I might have some trouble explaining the gun, the duct tape, and the shovel." He let loose a little giggle. "It would certainly make things interesting."

And then Joseph saw her. The third donor. He knew it was her right away. Middle-aged, a little bit overweight, and pushing a shopping cart full of God-knows-what down the side of the street.

Joseph slowed his car to a crawl and rolled down the front passenger window. "Excuse me, I'm sorry, but I was wondering if you could help me?" he mock-pleaded. The woman with the ratty graying hair and bright green eyes stopped walking but didn't respond. Joseph tried again.

"I'm new to the city (*which was true*) and extremely lost (*not true*). I'm really hoping you can help me (*true*) find the address where I'm supposed to go (*not true*). I have a really big meeting and I'm going to be late (*definitely not true*)."

The homeless woman continued to stare at Joseph with her piercing green eyes, but now there was a hint of curiosity breaking through too. The doctor played his final card. He knew if this one didn't work then he'd need to move on, just in case people here had been warned about a lingering silver sedan.

"Look, it's starting to rain. Why don't you just sit in the passenger seat while you help me with the map? It won't take long, I promise. I'll pay you for your help," Joseph lied. He smiled and held up both of his hands in a pretend show of benevolence. "I won't hurt you, I swear."

That part is true, Joseph thought. *One bullet to the head and she'll die instantly. No pain. No hurt.*

The stranger's promise of money and brief shelter from the rain was what finally convinced Hillary to let go of her shopping cart, open the car door, and lower herself down into the passenger seat. People didn't usually ask her for help – it was always the other way around. But she could use all of the money she could get, and this fella seemed nice enough. He didn't look crazy or anything like that. Especially not when he smiled.

"Where is it that you need to get to?" Hillary asked as she looked at the city map that Joseph had just passed over. Unbeknownst to her, the map had been purchased less than ten minutes earlier at a gas station right off the interstate.

"Blue Mountain National Park," Joseph responded coolly, clicking the doors locked as he spoke.

The woman's once curious green eyes were now full of fear as the man in the driver's seat moved his right foot from brake to gas and began to take her away from the streets that had been her home for the past nine years. Hillary had been married before that to a lousy, drunken excuse for a husband. He'd hit her way too many times for Hillary to keep his name after he died of alcohol poisoning, and she'd been in the foster system her entire childhood so she didn't really have a family from which she could take a surname. So she just went by Hillary. And right now Hillary was absolutely petrified.

"Y-you aren't lost-t, a-are you?" the involuntary blood donor stuttered.

"What gave it away?" a smirking Joseph replied. "The fact that the national park is nowhere near where you were? Or how about that the car is moving?" He chuckled. "You know, if you had half a brain, you might have figured it out when someone like me stopped to ask someone like you for directions. When I offered to let someone like you disgrace my car with your filthy presence. But, then again," Joseph added as he reached into the middle console and pulled out his gun, "if you had half a brain you also probably wouldn't be living on the streets, would you?"

Hillary opened her mouth to respond, to defend herself, to explain to her captor that she had always made A's and B's in school but was never able to stay in a foster home long enough to put together a good transcript. But the sharp jut of Joseph's gun into her ribcage prevented any response on her part.

"You know, I like you better than the last one," Joseph admitted as he drove back west in the direction of his murdering grounds. "He talked way too much."

The tear that had escaped Hillary's eye rolled into her mouth when she gasped at the madman's comment. *The last one. There were more.* The tears began to flow more steadily now. *He's going to kill me.*

FIVE

"Can't you dig any faster?" Joseph complained angrily. They had already passed the two hour mark, which was the time in which both of his previous homeless helpers had dug their graves. It would be getting dark soon.

The duct tape across Hillary's mouth kept her from issuing an answer.

"C'mon woman. The rain should've softened up the ground for you. Put your back into it." Joseph shook his head in frustration. *This is what happens when you ask a woman to do something. Too damn slow*, he thought.

****

Forty-five minutes later, nearly three hours after Hillary first put shovel to dirt, her hole was complete.

"Finally!" Joseph exclaimed. "I know I said earlier that I liked you better than the last guy, but he didn't take three damn hours to dig a four foot hole." He pursed his lips together and shook his head back and forth. "You've lost most favored status, my dear."

A pair of exhausted green eyes stared back at Joseph in disbelief. *What the hell is this guy's problem?* Hillary thought. *Most favored status? He ranks his victims? Frickin' psycho.*

Joseph scratched his head with the business end of his pistol. "Not as if I owe you anything, but I want to explain my reasoning before I shoot you. Because some people should know the full truth." Joseph paused before adding: "not that you'll live long enough to tell anyone."

Hillary simply sighed, part exhaustion and part resignation. *That's what you get for getting in the car with a stranger.* Hillary's longtime social worker's warnings about 'stranger danger' suddenly came flooding back into her mind – approximately four hours too late.

Joseph's next words brought Hillary back to the present. "I'm a doctor," he declared with pride. "A brilliant doctor. But for some reason that I will never understand, people don't seem to realize that I am a national treasure. A once-in-a-generation mind. And America is going to find out what happens when you don't take care of your national treasures. When people who could work for good decide to focus on . . . *other* pursuits."

The woman standing in front of Joseph had begun to shiver as he spoke; the cold from the rain combining with drying sweat from the three hours spent digging her own grave.

"Close your eyes. Or turn around or something," Joseph suddenly commanded. "The green color of your eyes is freaking me out."

Hillary did as she was told and turned around, putting her back to her captor. There was no point resisting now. This nut job doctor had driven her out into the middle of a national park (if he was telling the truth about that), made her dig a hole with a shovel for nearly three hours straight, and was now waving a gun around as he spoke. *Even if I did manage to escape, I'm too damn tired to get very far. I'd probably die of exposure or get eaten by a wild animal. At least this way, with this crazy guy and his gun, I know how I'll go*, she thought sadly.

The last thing Hillary heard was Joseph's laugh.

****

Joseph quickly removed the layers of jackets and sweaters that the newly-dead woman at his feet had been wearing, trying to uncover her arms so he could begin draining her blood. Much to his surprise, his third and final donor wasn't overweight at all. In fact, she was mere skin and bones. "No wonder it took you so long to dig the hole," Joseph muttered as he pulled the last sweater up and over Hillary's lifeless head. "There's not an ounce of muscle on you."

Disgusted with himself for his choice of victim, Joseph began inserting needles into the body's bony arms. "There's no way I get a full twelve pints out of you. I'll be lucky if I get ten."

Thick red blood began to flow out of Hillary's veins and into the plastic pouches on the ground of the grave below her as Joseph finally let himself relax a little bit. *It'll be fine*, he told himself. *A couple less pints of blood than we planned on isn't the end of the world. We'll still have enough.*

SIX

It didn't occur to Joseph that perhaps his perception of all homeless people as drug-addicted miscreants was disproven by the fact that all three of his involuntary blood donors tested negative for any drugs in their system. Joseph had screened the blood to make sure it was usable, since it didn't matter that his virus was undetectable if the blood was going to be thrown out for traces of meth or crack or hepatitis or whatever else those people got themselves into. *Well*, he thought as he watched a small centrifuge spin on his worktable, *I guess I got lucky. The black guy did have alcohol in his system, but that's easy enough to flush out.* Which was what he was doing at that moment. In essence, washing Willie 'Shoes' McRae's blood so it would come back clean when or if the Red Cross or hospitals tested it.

A small buzzer sounded to signal that the centrifuge had stopped spinning. "All done!" Joseph said gleefully as he opened the lid of the cylinder-shaped machine and pulled out the final remaining vials of Donor Number Two's blood. Walking over to the refrigerator where all of the virus ingredients were being stored, he continued: "now all we have to do is mix everything together and it'll be ready for delivery!"

****

"Are you baking a cake?"

Joseph froze. He was used to hearing voices while he worked in his secret laboratory, but they were always the ones inside his own head. They were never from someone else. And they *definitely* were never in the form of an elementary school-aged girl who literally had pigtails in her hair.

"Peyton," Joseph hissed under his breath as he remained standing with his back to the direction where the voice came from.

"Mr. Joseph? Did you hear me? I asked if you were baking a cake."

The mad scientist closed his eyes and literally felt a growl rise up in his throat. He hadn't imagined it. The little brat of a child from down the street – the one who had made it her mission to befriend the reclusive doctor – was standing on what sounded like the top step leading from his kitchen into his secret lair. The secret lair where he had out, in plain view, bags full of human blood and vials full of a virus the likes of which the world had never seen.

Breathe, Joseph commanded himself. *At the very least, she's still in a position where she could escape. Breathe, he seethed. Be nice.*

Freshly-cleaned blood still in hand, Joseph slowly turned around and tried his best to smile.

"Why, Miss Finch, what a surprise."

The little girl gave him a toothy grin and appeared genuinely happy to see Joseph. Exactly why that was he would never understand. Taking his smile and opening comment as an invitation, the gangly blonde with a ribbon in each pigtail slowly climbed down the rest of the stairs until her feet were planted firmly in the room that housed Joseph's most evil machinations.

"So what are you making?" the girl asked again. "I heard you say it will be ready for delivery soon."

"And how do you know what 'ready for delivery' means?"

Peyton Finch put her hands on her hips and looked at him incredulously. "I'm eight, not three," she declared in a huff. "And I'm a Girl Scout. We deliver cookies . . . *duh*. I came to see if you wanted to buy any."

The girl's brief display of disrespect was the straw that broke the camel's already very weak back. Joseph had labeled his entire viral scheme Operation Respect, and he would be damned if he was going to let this little punk get away with talking to him like that.

Without even trying to be subtle about it, Joseph turned back around, placed the cleaned blood in the refrigerator, closed the door, and then pressed a large red button on the concrete wall that caused the trap door to his underground lab to immediately snap shut.

Peyton jumped in surprise.

"I'm making a virus," Joseph said as he slowly turned to face his young intruder. This time he made no effort to appear friendly; instead, the evil gleam in his eyes and grin on his face were the same ones that his three homeless victims had seen shortly before they met their Maker.

The only child of Jim and Marie Finch began to slowly back away from Joseph, suddenly afraid of the neighbor with whom she had so desperately wanted to be friends.

"Where are you going, Peyton?" Joseph mocked as he matched the little girl step for step. "There's no way out now." His grin turned into a full smile and he chuckled, genuinely enjoying this moment. "You know you've been a pain in the ass ever since you got old enough to walk down to my house. Always knocking on my door." Joseph paused as something occurred to him. "How did you get inside anyway?"

"I . . . I . . .," she stuttered, "I went through the back d-door. It was unl-locked."

Joseph cursed his complacency under his breath. He knew he should have never left any of his doors unlocked. *Especially* when he was working in his lab.

"You know what that's called?" Joseph asked, transferring his anger from himself to his young neighbor. "Trespassing. Didn't your parents ever teach you not to go into other people's houses uninvited?"

The third-grader simply lowered her head and gently stubbed her sneaker-clad toe into the concrete floor.

"Answer me!" Joseph bellowed.

"Y-y-yes," Peyton stammered as tears began to fall down her cheeks. "T-t-they d-did."

Joseph expelled a deep, frustrated breath and ran his hand through his short hair. "You see, Peyton, I have a problem now. I was having a really good Saturday until you showed up. And now I have a problem." He then walked over to a second small refrigerator and pulled out a syringe. As he lightly tapped the side of the clear tube with his finger, the doctor added:

"Here's my problem. If I was a trusting person," – otherwise known as an idiot, he thought – "I would just make you promise to never ever tell anyone what you saw today."

The little girl's eyes grew bigger with every step that Joseph and the large needle made in her direction.

"But I don't trust you," he added. The thought briefly crossed his mind that if she were older, right now would be the time when Peyton would start pleading her case and declaring that she would never ever tell a soul that she had even gone to her neighbor Joseph's house. But the owner of the pigtails didn't start begging for him to trust her. She just stood there. Terrified.

The doctor used the non-needle end of the syringe to scratch his forehead. "And because I don't trust you, the only solution I can see is that I have to kill you."

A deluge of tears now made their way down the young girl's face. All she had wanted to do was ask Mr. Joseph to buy a box or two of cookies. And now he just said he was going to kill her.

"What, no reply?" a confident Joseph asked. "I wish the others had been as compliant as you."

Peyton didn't know who 'the others' were; neither did she know what the word compliant meant. But it didn't sound good.

"Oh, for God's sake. Say something!" ordered the man with the syringe full of an unknown liquid. "Say anything."

Even in the small room, Joseph had to strain to hear Peyton's whispered reply: "p-please don't kill me."

SEVEN

Joseph had never liked actors; never thought that their work of entertaining people was valuable in the least. In fact, he usually viewed the entire modern entertainment industry as a bad thing – a behemoth of a movement that only served to distract people from productive work. But right now, in this moment, the scheming doctor wished he had taken acting classes. Wished he had done high school drama or something, *anything*, to help him pull off the hoax Joseph had concocted in his head after injecting little Peyton with enough tranquilizer to keep her unconscious for at least twenty-four hours.

His plan was to wait until it got dark and drive the girl out to the same spot where he killed the three homeless people. Once there, Joseph would shoot Peyton, drain her blood, and bury her – making her death look just like the others. It was his only option. He couldn't kill the girl in his house because it would leave too much evidence. Joseph could explain away the safe room-turned-lab if the police searched his house and he had to, but you can't explain away blood spatter or any of the other inevitable traces of evidence left behind at murder scenes.

Right now, however, Joseph needed to start building up a good image with Jim and Marie Finch so they – and, more importantly, the police – wouldn't suspect him of any wrongdoing. Which was why Joseph found himself picking a ten dollar bill out of his wallet, exiting his front door, and walking down his quiet suburban street in the direction of the Finch house.

****

After he rang the doorbell of the house where Peyton would no longer live, Joseph took a deep breath and told himself to think happy thoughts. Whereas most people would envision puppies or kittens, Joseph saw himself at a banquet accepting an award for his groundbreaking work in pathology. He smiled.

Marie Finch opened the front door with a puzzled yet friendly expression on her face. "Joseph. Hi. To what do I owe the surprise?"

The doctor continued to smile for the benefit of his act. *Step One*, Joseph thought. *Establish that you think the girl is still alive, safe and sound, even when she's not.* He finally answered: "I actually came over to see Peyton. She stopped by my house earlier selling Girl Scout cookies, and I ordered a few boxes but didn't have any cash on me. I told her I would come over later after I had gone to the ATM."

The school nurse gave him the same exaggerated look of disappointment that she often directed at students when telling them something that wasn't really that big of a deal. "Oh, I'm so sorry. I got a text from her about an hour ago saying she was going to play at the creek with some neighborhood kids. But I'll be happy to take the money and put it with the rest of her orders."

As he handed Mrs. Finch the $10, Joseph began Step Two: *Act like you don't know she has a cell phone.* Which wasn't true – Joseph was the one who sent the text message about the creek. He beamed inwardly with pride . . . *I'm so smart I scare myself sometimes.*

Joseph issued a little laugh and shook his head in mock disbelief. "An eight-year-old with a cell phone. Kids these days."

Peyton's mother smiled a smile that didn't quite reach her eyes, taking the neighbor's comment as an attack on her parenting. "It's a whole new world out there," was all she could manage to say.

Not yet, Joseph thought, *but it will be once I'm through with it. And now it's time for Step Three: reiterate your belief in the young girl's safety.*

"Indeed it is," he lied in response to the woman's last, 'new world' comment. "Well, I don't want to take up any more of your time. Just be sure to tell Peyton that I did bring the money by."

"I will," Mrs. Finch assured him as she took a step back and closed the door.

This time Joseph was the one truly smiling. "Success!" he said gleefully as he made his way back home.

****

If an eight-year-old little girl doesn't come home when she is supposed to, her parents get worried. They call their neighbors, who join in worrying. And before long the entire street of moms and dads is out searching for one of their own. Joseph expected the neighbors to come to his front door to tell him what was going on, but the knock surprisingly never came.

Joseph heard the first yells of "Peyton!" outside the front of his house about three hours after he returned from his visit with Mrs. Finch. Unbeknownst to the search party, the little girl was in a peaceful, tranquilizer-induced sleep in their reclusive neighbor's safe room-turned-lab.

"Peyton!" the yells continued. "This isn't funny, Peyton!"

Joseph wasn't known on the neighborhood street for being particularly friendly – in fact, he was known for being rather gruff and a loner – but there was no way he could ignore the hunt for Peyton Finch. Not without arousing suspicion, anyway. So the doctor donned his windbreaker, grabbed his cell phone, and walked outside.

"Hey, what's going on?" he asked as innocently as he could.

A man from a few houses down, someone who Joseph had probably met before but hadn't cared about enough to remember his name, looked over at Joseph and answered: "the Finch girl has gone missing. She told her parents she was going to play at the creek but she's not there. They can't find her anywhere."

"Peyton Finch?" Joseph asked, feigning worry. "Has anyone called the police?" *Yeah, that's good*, he thought to himself. *Volunteer the idea of involving the police . . . no guilty person would do that.*

"I don't know," the neighbor replied. "I think so. Probably. I would have if it were my kid," he rambled on.

"What can I do to help?" Joseph asked, again trying to blend in with the reaction of everyone else in the neighborhood.

The other man paused for a minute, obviously surprised by the usually anti-social doctor's offer to assist in the search.

Joseph sensed the reason behind his neighbor's delay and offered: "look, I know I'm not the most outgoing of people and I don't really socialize with any of you because you're all married with children and I'm not, but that doesn't mean I'm some evil guy who won't help look for a little girl who is missing."

The neighbor nodded his head. "You're right. I'm sorry. Obviously you can join the search. We're just fanning out through the area looking for her. We're thinking she might have fallen and hurt herself somehow."

"Okay. I'll start looking around in the woods behind my house first and go from there." Joseph then turned and walked away in the direction he had indicated, very proud of himself for his sublime acting performance. *Now I just help search until they call it off on account of darkness, and then get rid of the little brat after everyone goes to sleep.*

Joseph chuckled to himself as he walked through the woods behind his house, calling out "Peyton!" every once in a while for good measure. *'We think she fell and hurt herself.' Ha. Nope! She's not hurt yet. But she will be soon enough.*

"Curiosity killed the cat," he mumbled, "and it killed the kid too."

EIGHT

"Damn," Joseph cursed aloud as a dirt-covered glove wiped sweat from his brow. "This is a lot harder than I thought."

'This' was the grave that he was digging for the pint-sized pain in the ass that lay unconscious inside a plastic tarp a few feet away from him. The M.O. for all four murders had to be the same: kidnapped, shot, blood drained, buried in the national park. "What does M.O. even stand for?" he wondered. "Ah, who gives a shit," he decided, his language worsening as he got more and more tired. "They all just have to be the same."

This might have been the first time that the doctor engaged in any serial killings, but he was no fool. He knew he had to cover his tracks with these murders, just like he did with the virus. Which was why he had taken the time to drive into the sketch part of the city and drop Peyton's bedazzled pink cell phone and one of her hair ribbons in a dumpster. Joseph knew that the police would trace the phone to the dumpster, "and that further removes any suspicion from any of the neighbors. Especially me." Again the man repeated two of his new life mottos.

"No body, no murder." Followed by: "Never leave a trail."

It took the evil genius a full two and a half hours for his skinny arms to dig a hole deep enough for little Miss Finch to hopefully stay buried forever. In a hurry to get this unfortunate detour over with and get back on track with his viral terrorism plans, Joseph quickly climbed out of the hole, shot the girl, drained her blood, and buried her in the hastily-prepared grave.

"And that," Joseph said as he brushed dirt off his clothes, "is why you don't go into people's homes uninvited."

****

The morning after Peyton's murder, Joseph sat at his kitchen table looking at a map of the United States. An old-fashioned paper Atlas. Not something online that the tech geeks with the police department could uncover, should it ever come to that. "Shit," Joseph exclaimed. "This is going to make things difficult."

Joseph was trying to figure out the best way to deliver his virus-tainted blood to its final destination. His first thought had been to fly, but there was no way he could explain a suitcase full of blood to the TSA. Next he considered shipping his accomplice and flying out to meet it, but then there would be a record of both the shipment and his flight travel. The only option Joseph really had was to drive. "But some of these delivery locations are really far away," he lamented.

Potential drop zone A would take a full twenty-four hours one way without any stops. Drop zone C was twelve hours. D would be seventeen. Eventually Joseph would narrow his choices down to three, knowing that it all had to be done over the weekends and before the blood got too old to use. "I can't take any time off of work. People might get suspicious. I can't leave a trail. Cannot leave a trail," the infectious disease expert muttered as he got up from the table, put the Atlas back in its drawer, and grabbed his car keys from a hook on the wall. It was time to make another cash withdrawal from the ATM. Joseph knew he would need a lot of cash for his journeys, but he was taking it out in small amounts over a long period of time so it wouldn't draw any unwanted attention.

"Can't leave a trail. Never leave a trail."

NINE

Joseph's heart was racing as he parked his car in front of the Red Cross Denver Regional Blood Bank. Over two years of planning, research, and preparation had gone into this project, and now it all came down to execution. The biggest variable, of course, was that the virus had never been tested on humans. But every dry run with the mice had gone exactly according to plan. And, in a last minute fit of panic, his decision to test the virus on a few cats had also worked well. A lesser man, a weaker man, a man not committed to his mission, might have felt sorry for the strays that Joseph snatched from behind a local seafood restaurant. But not Joseph. "No regrets," he said as he took a deep breath and exited the car.

****

"Here, let me help you with those," the pretty blonde receptionist offered as Joseph pushed open the door to the blood storage facility and attempted to carry a large box through the doorway.

"Thank you very much," Joseph responded, genuinely grateful for the assistance. The Red Cross-labeled climate-controlled box that he was carrying was a lot heavier than expected, especially when he was so tired from the long drive from home to here.

The receptionist – her nametag read 'Severin' – held the door open for Joseph as he finally managed to maneuver the large box through the doorframe. "Dropping off?" the young woman asked.

Joseph carefully set the container full of virus-tainted blood pouches on the ground and took a deep breath. *It's showtime*, he thought as he stood up to face the girl.

"Yep, dropping off."

"Great," Severin exclaimed cheerfully. "We always need more donations." She then walked back over to the desk in the middle of the foyer and picked up a clipboard with a piece of paper attached to it. "If you just fill out this form here, I can get the blood all entered into our system and you can be on your way."

Shit, Joseph thought. *I knew I would forget something. Of course they aren't going to just let me drop off a bunch of blood without any sort of record attached to it.*

"Form?" he asked, trying desperately to stall for time while masking the panic in his voice.

"Yep," the receptionist answered, her curly hair bouncing up and down as she nodded her head. "It's really short. You just fill in the blanks with the blood drive location and number of donors and all that. Doesn't take long at all." Severin paused. "Have you never done this before?"

Not wanting to raise any suspicion, Joseph quickly grabbed at the convenient excuse that the receptionist had just offered him. "No," he answered, shaking his head back and forth, "I'm new. This is my first time running a blood drive."

The peppy blonde seemed to accept Joseph's answer without any further curiosity. "No worries, it's really simple. And if you have any questions about the form you can just ask me."

If their conversation had been via email or text, Joseph imagined that Severin would have added a sideways smiley face to the end of her sentence. *I don't understand how people can be that happy all of the time*, he thought. *She's like a freaking smile factory.*

Putting aside his growing irritation with the young woman for her grave error of simply being nice, Joseph took the clipboard that he was handed and began to fill in his made-up answers.

Name . . . umm . . . , Joseph racked his brain for something to write. Spontaneous creativity was definitely not his strong suit. *Draw on your own life experiences. C'mon, Joe. You can do this.* He settled on Mark Quinton, the name of his first college roommate.

Home address? Ah hell.

1234 Maple Lane, Denver, CO.

Shit. I don't know the zip code here. Joseph quickly scanned the information form for any kind of office address. Luckily, he found one running along the very bottom of the page, in a font so small he could barely read it.

80219.

Location of blood drive? Double shit.

"Excuse me, Severin?" Joseph asked as politely and innocently as he knew how. "I don't remember the actual address of where we did the blood drive."

"Oh, don't worry about that part," she answered dismissively. "Just write in the name of the school or wherever you did it. I mean, to be honest with you," Severin added, "nobody ever really checks those things. We're just required to attach it to the box. The most important thing is that you put the right date on there so we don't use blood that has expired."

Joseph breathed a massive internal sigh of relief. He had envisioned people double-checking his home address (*is there even a Maple Lane in Denver?*) and calling the location to see if there had been a blood drive that day. That would've ended his project before it ever even began. Joseph smiled at the girl whose pretty blonde curls were beginning to grow on him.

"Oh, great," he responded genuinely. The young woman went back to whatever she was doing on the computer – *probably checking Facebook*, Joseph thought – while the doctor resumed filling out the donation form.

Location of the blood drive?

Parking lot of a Target store.

Number of units donated? Here we go, Joseph thought. *I know these answers.*

In the space under units donated he put twelve, trying his best to not write using the chicken scratch that could have been used to identify him as a doctor. He then added the day's date and scribbled a signature where required, which ended up being nothing more than an M and a Q with a squiggly line after each.

God, I hope Mark Quinton doesn't work for the Red Cross, he silently prayed. Joseph wasn't one to pray very often; he wasn't one to acknowledge the existence of a being higher than himself very often, but this was one of those rare moments. Joseph also superstitiously crossed two fingers on his free hand as he passed the clipboard and its accompanying form full of lies back to the receptionist. "All done," he announced.

"Great!" Severin answered as she reached up and took the materials from Joseph. "See, I told you it wouldn't take long."

Does this girl ever stop smiling? The crossed fingers morphed into a clinched fist, a reminder from Joseph to himself to keep his emotions in check. He had never had much in the way of a filter on his speech – whatever he thought he usually said, regardless of its level of appropriateness – but he knew that he needed a filter right now. One wrong move, one snarky comment, and this whole endeavor could blow up in his face.

Taking a deep breath, Joseph finally replied: "nope, it was painless." Then, gesturing to the box at his feet, he added: "what do I do with the blood?"

"Oh, you can just leave that there," answered Severin. "I'll put all of this information into the computer and then have somebody from the back come up and get it."

"Okay. So I'm done?"

"Yep, you're all set. Unless there's anything else I can do for you?"

"No, that was it," Joseph replied. "Thanks."

The scheming doctor heard the receptionist call out "have a nice day," but he didn't turn around or return the valediction. At that moment Joseph had only one objective: to get the hell out of there before the blonde girl started typing his answers into her computer and it kicked back 'ADDRESS NOT FOUND.'

TEN

"Country. Country. Country." Joseph's voice grew more and more irritated with each push of the radio dial button as he drove away from the Colorado Red Cross facility. "Doesn't anyone here listen to anything else aside from country music?"

The answer, unfortunately for Joseph, was no. He had his iPod connected to the car's sound system, but after listening to all of those songs four times in a row, the virus-maker was desperately in need of some fresh tunes.

Finally, in frustration, he simply turned the radio completely off. He liked a fairly good variety of music, but country just did not make the cut. The twang, the sappy stories, the endless talk of family, beer, and Jesus . . . it was all too much heartland America for the agnostic city kid. But where he was driving at the moment was the heartland – *also known as the middle of nowhere*, he thought – and country music was pretty much Joseph's only option.

"It's alright," the slender man said aloud. The stress of the past couple of weeks had caused him to lose a good deal of weight and added more than a few new gray hairs to his head. Joseph did a lot of talking to his windshield these days. "I'm learning a lot on this first drop off. Things I will need to know for the next two. Like having my background story prepared and ready to go in case they ask. And stocking up on Red Bull before I start driving." He laughed as more things started coming to mind. "I really am a rookie at this. I need to bring a pillow and a blanket in case I want to stop and take a nap on the way. A car-charger for my phone . . . that thing's been dead since God knows when yesterday. And, how could I have ever forgotten, I need to invest in satellite radio. Or books on tape. Maybe both." Joseph shook his head. "I cannot spend hours upon hours listening to country music. And I'm sure that's all there is on the way to Nashville."

The Nashville blood drop would be Joseph's third and final trip, after this weekend in Colorado and then New York City next weekend.

So far so good, though, he thought. *A full one-third of the virus is now in play.* That realization suddenly made him a little bit nervous. Ever since Joseph first came up with his virus scheme, ever since he first concocted Operation Respect, everything had been under his control. But once he put the tainted blood out there, there was nothing else he could do. *I'll just have to sit back and wait for the results.*

****

Joseph was prepared this time. One week after the near-disaster in Colorado, he was ready. He had the fake name, the fake donation location; he had even practiced his fake signature for the forms he would have to sign at the blood bank. *I'm ready,* Joseph thought with confidence.

The regional blood bank in Denver had been very nice. Big, clean, obviously a new facility with plenty of parking and a front desk worker who was very easy on the eyes. But this place? *The exact opposite,* thought Joseph has he shouldered open the rundown building's heavy front door. The Red Cross' regional blood distribution center for the mid-Atlantic and New England was in an old warehouse-looking place in Queens, and Joseph felt like he was going to catch a disease just pushing the button to call the elevator. Precariously balancing the heavy box of blood on his khaki-clad knee, the doctor took another look around. *I guess this is all a non-profit can afford in the New York market.*

The elevator doors opened on the sixth floor and Joseph quickly saw that looks could be deceiving, since while the outside and lobby of the building appeared rather run-down, the floor actually occupied by the Red Cross was pristine. Freshly-painted white walls, clean carpet, and what looked like the same poster-sized pictures that had been hanging in the Denver office. Smiling patients with doctors and nurses wearing Red Cross arm bands. *I really hope they didn't pay someone to come up with that as a marketing idea,* Joseph thought, getting in one last snarky moment before descending into full nice guy mode. *You're here to drop off blood that will save people's lives! Hooray!* Joseph mentally instructed himself. He then adjusted his grip on the box he was carrying, adorned with the same fake Red Cross labels that he had slapped on the first donation box, and proceeded forward out of the elevator toward the IKEA-like table that was serving as the receptionist's desk.

Except there was no receptionist. Having planned his entire speech from beginning to end, Joseph wasn't prepared to find no one waiting to greet him.

"Uh . . . hello?" he called out. "Is there anybody here?"

Joseph heard footsteps and then a man's voice answering him. "Yeah, hold on, I'm comin'."

In that instant, Joseph found himself wishing this office had a receptionist like the one in Denver. Sure, he had found Severin's perky happiness to be supremely annoying, but at least she hadn't ever addressed him in a tone that made it sound like Joseph was bothering her. *New Yorkers,* he thought with a derisive huff.

A short, balding man with a terrible comb-over and obvious membership to the Fast Food Lovers of America and Twinkie of the Month clubs finally rounded the corner of an office cubicle, panting from the exertion of walking there from wherever he was before. Joseph tried to hide his disgust at the man's appearance, having no patience for people who were overweight. He thought extra pounds meant a person was lazy, and their overconsumption of food made them a drag on the nation's productivity and resources.

"Sorry 'bout that," the staffer said in a heavy accent, wiping his sweaty brow with a handkerchief. 'I was way back in the back." Glancing at the box in Joseph's rapidly tiring hands, he added: "you heeuh to drop that off?"

Joseph wanted nothing more than to answer back, "no, I just like to carry this around for the hell of it." But he didn't. *I'm a nice person. I'm a volunteer. I'm helping the Red Cross*, he mentally reminded himself in a voice that sounded a lot like young Peyton Finch once did. Instead, the schemer simply answered: "yeah."

The Red Cross staffer, name-tagged 'Tony,' was clearly preoccupied. "Alright, look, you done this beforah?" he asked. It was a struggle to understand everything that this Tony character said, but when Joseph nodded his head in the affirmative, the New Yorker continued: "okay, look, I'm the only one heeuh tuhday. Jus' leave the box theyah, write the date and numbuh of units on it, and I'll get to it laytuh."

Part of Joseph was happy that were would be no checking of names or addresses, but another part of him was pissed that he wasted so much time making up a cover story that he didn't need. And the mad scientist definitely didn't like the idea of his prized virus sitting out in the open for anyone to come by and steal.

"Shouldn't we at least move the blood behind the desk or something so it's not just out here in the middle of the floor?" Joseph asked.

"Yeah, let's do that," the worker agreed. He then walked up beside Joseph, bent down, and pushed the container across the carpeted floor to where it was hidden behind the desk. Preoccupied by whatever he had been doing before, Tony then turned to leave. "Like I said, jus' put the date and how much blood it is on the box theyah. Thanks fuh the donation."

And just like that, Joseph once again found himself alone in the reception area, the staffer having quickly waddled back around the corner and out of sight. The doctor shook his head in disbelief at how smoothly today's drop-off had gone. "The blood supply is even easier to infiltrate than I thought it would be," he muttered as he quickly grabbed a marker from the desk and wrote "twelve units" and the day's date on top of the box.

Joseph had collected thirty-six units in all – twelve from the first two homeless men, ten from the scrawny third 'donor,' and two from himself. He then mixed the one-pint bags so that each donation box would have a variety of blood types in it. A box full of blood that was all the same type might raise suspicion. But by sheer luck, the three homeless murder victims all had different types of blood – A-positive, B-negative, and AB-negative – and Joseph's universal donor O-negative added in made it a great mix. Joseph had thought about adding Peyton's blood as well, but in the end he didn't do so simply because he didn't have enough of the virus. In order for it to work properly, Joseph had to give each pint of blood a fairly concentrated dose of his deadly mixture, and there simply wasn't any more left over to include Peyton with the group. Consequently, each of the three chosen drop locations would only receive twelve units, and hopefully those units would be distributed far and wide. Joseph wanted his virus to make as big of an impact as possible, *and the best way to do that will be to have the whole country scared shitless that they might be the next one to be infected*, he thought with a smile.

After he finished writing on the box, Joseph stood up and arched his back to stretch. He still had a long drive ahead of him to get back home. Working all week and then travelling each weekend to drop off his next supply of blood was certainly taking its toll on his middle-aged body.

Only one more after this, Joseph thought with relief. *Only one more.*

****

Joseph's experience in New York City didn't sit well with him. He didn't like the way that Tony character treated him and his virus. As if they were . . . not important. Wasting Tony's time. Not worthy of respect. Joseph didn't like it when people didn't respect him. A thought also continued to haunt Joseph: what happened to his box of donated blood? The Red Cross office had been rather deserted, but what if some random showed up, saw the box unattended, and stole it? Even if the person didn't know what they were stealing, losing a full one-third of his virus would definitely affect how much of an impact Operation Respect would have around the country. The entire mid-Atlantic and Northeast, America's most populous region, would be taken out of play.

The virus' architect carried his worries to the office with him that next week, despite Joseph's best attempts to separate his 'day job' from his work on Operation Respect. He was more-than-slightly paranoid that someone, somehow, would notice a difference in his attitude or actions, notice would turn to suspicion, and suspicion would turn to investigation – with the entire enterprise crumbling down around him. Nevertheless, Joseph couldn't help but worry about what happened in New York. Couldn't help but wonder if everything he had been working towards for the past two years was going to fail because of some overweight, sweaty, lower-class slacker in Queens.

"Are you alright?" The question was directed at Joseph by one of his most trusted lab assistants. The woman had a worried expression on her face, which in turn caused a worried expression to ripple through Joseph's body.

"What? Why? Of course I'm alright," Joseph responded with more than a little gruff defensiveness.

His officemate wasn't deterred. "You just seem like your mind has been somewhere else these past few days."

It took all of the inner fortitude that Joseph could muster to not snap back at the curious doctor standing in front of him. *Be cool*, he reminded himself. *Don't arouse suspicion. Just be cool.* Taking a deep breath, Joseph answered: "I'm just juggling a lot of different projects right now. I'm fine."

When he could see that she wasn't completely satisfied with his answer, Joseph added: "maybe if you spent a little less time worrying about me and a little more time worrying about your work, you'd be further along with that new vaccine."

The lab assistant was smart enough to know when to back off. Shoving her hands down into the pockets of her lab coat, the woman simply nodded her head and replied "okay" before turning around and walking back to her workstation.

Once he was satisfied that his officemate had returned her attention to her work instead of her boss, Joseph unleashed a torrent of nasty attacks on himself. *Get your fucking act together, Joe*, he began. *You're so caught up in worrying about that idiot in New York ruining things that you're going to be the one to screw it all up. New York is done. It's out of your hands. Leave it and move on.*

But Joseph knew he wouldn't just leave it and move on. He couldn't. When he was truly honest with himself, Joseph admitted that what happened in New York had bothered him so much because it reminded him of his relationship with his parents. So many times as a boy, young Joseph would come home from school with exciting things to tell his mom and dad – only to be brushed off as not important enough or interesting enough for their attention. *Children should be seen and not heard, boy*, was one of Joseph Sr.'s favorite lines when speaking to his son. When he took the time to speak to the boy at all, that is. Joseph's mother was no better; so meek and timid and in awe of her husband that her only child barely registered in her thoughts.

Yes, it was painful and a touch embarrassing to admit – even to himself – but Joseph hadn't liked Tony in New York because Tony in New York was just as dismissive toward him as Joseph Sr. had been. As if it was a chore to have to spend any time around him.

The unexpected feeling of wetness filling his eyes and his throat tightening caused Joseph to break out of his thoughts. *Get a grip, Joe*, he told himself as he cleared his throat and quickly blinked away what had been rapidly approaching tears. *This is a medical research lab, not a therapist's couch. Man up, do your work, and stop blubbering like a teenage girl.*

The pep talk and the horrific thought that someone might have actually noticed him crying were enough to get Joseph's head back on straight. Or at least as straight as a man like him's head could ever be.

ELEVEN

Nashville, Tennessee, as Joseph discovered the next weekend, is a lovely city. The people are friendly, the weather is nice, and the music scene adds a unique layer of culture that pervades most everything. Just north of the vibrant city center, in a suburb called Bellshire Terrace, was where Joseph found his third and final regional blood donation center. The Red Cross' southeast blood hub occupied one of the anchor units of a strip mall that had obviously seen better days, having been hit hard by both the economic recession and the opening of a Wal-Mart just down the street. There were few cars in the parking lot when Joseph arrived shortly before noon on Saturday, and he had his pick of parking spaces right in front of the Red Cross office's doors.

Grateful to not have to carry the heavy box full of blood any farther than necessary, and happy to be completing the final step of his Operation Respect mission, Joseph bounded out of his car and quickly went around to the back to retrieve the blood box from his trunk. Happiness was not a feeling that Joseph experienced very often, but he wore it well today. The satellite radio subscription that he purchased earlier in the week had saved him from exposure to the South's affinity for country music, and the Red Bull he chugged about an hour earlier had his mind and body running on all cylinders. *Today is a good day*, Joseph thought as he carried the Styrofoam box away from his car. *It's going to be a very good day.*

A little bell attached to the front door rang to announce Joseph's entrance, and a cheerful woman who appeared to be in her early sixties looked up from her desk computer and smiled. "Hi there," the woman said in a deep Southern drawl. "Welcome to the Red Cross. My name is Suzanne. How can I help you?"

Despite his good mood, Joseph was a bit disconcerted by the bubbly woman seated at the desk in front of him. Her obviously dyed hair was a pale blonde, her makeup was well done (albeit a little too caked-on in his opinion), and she looked a lot like Paula Deen without the apron. In fact, what was probably the most disconcerting to Joseph was that this woman gave him a flash vision of what the worker in Denver, Severin, might look like in forty years. *What do they do? Specially recruit these people?* he thought.

"Sir?" the receptionist called out again. "Can I help you?"

Joseph quickly shook his head to bring his thoughts back to the task at hand. "Yes, I'm sorry. I was thinking about something else." He set the heavy box down on the floor and then stood up before continuing: "I'm here to drop off some blood from a donation drive."

Suzanne smiled in understanding. "Oh, no need to apologize darlin'. My mind is always goin' in a million directions at once." The woman started rummaging around in her desk drawers. "Now where are you comin' from hun'?"

Just as he had been last week in New York, Joseph was ready with his fake story. It was a good thing, too, since this Suzanne woman looked like the kind who might actually follow protocol and double-check his information.

"We were over at the Wal-Mart in Madison yesterday afternoon and this morning," Joseph began. "Not all that big of a turnout . . . we only collected twelve units."

"Oh that's okay," Suzanne replied, waving her hand dismissively. "Every little bit helps." Having found what she was looking for in her desk, the receptionist attached the blank donation form to a clipboard and handed it to Joseph. "I'm sure you've done this before, darlin', but I'll just need you to fill out this form so I can get everythin' put into our computers."

"Sure thing," Joseph replied in an unusually cheerful voice. He was acting, trying to match Suzanne's friendly nature, but it wasn't as difficult today given his happy mood. Taking the clipboard from the receptionist, he started to fill in the blanks.

Name?

Jim Finch. *A nice little tribute to Peyton*, Joseph thought with a grin.

Address? Ha, I'm ready for that one. He had gone online to find a random house, wanting to make sure that the address he gave these people actually existed. 1234 Maple Lane in Denver, much to his chagrin, did not exist.

Joseph wrote down: 351 Cumberland Hills Drive, Madison, TN 37125.

Location of blood drive?

Wal-Mart in Madison.

The number of units donated was twelve, and the day's date was easy enough. Joseph was a little bit worried about using blood that was now almost three weeks old, but he really didn't have a choice in the matter. It shouldn't cause any problems, provided this blood was sent to hospitals and used without too much further delay. As a doctor, Joseph was fully aware of the studies showing problems that could arise from giving people donated blood after it reached its so-called expiration date. But this blood was just now nearing three weeks post-"donation," and most of the problems happened once blood hit the one month or even six week mark. *It'll be fine. It will have to be fine*, Joseph told himself. *Besides, even if this blood is a little bit too old, it shouldn't do anything to counteract the virus . . . if anything it will just make the impact a little bit different than in the mice trials.*

"All done?" the bottle-blonde Suzanne asked when she saw that Joseph had stopped writing.

"Oh, yep," Joseph answered.

"You are a bit of a scatter-brain, aren't you, dear?" the woman in front of him said with a gentle laugh. Joseph wasn't really sure what to think of her repeatedly calling him things like "darlin" and "dear," but he figured it must be a Southern thing. *Just like the guy in New York didn't know how to use an R in his words.*

The doctor in disguise tried his best to improvise an answer. "I'm not usually this bad," he said with a smile. "I must just be getting hungry or something."

Suzanne looked at the slender gold watch on her wrist. "Oh goodness, it is almost lunch time isn't it? Well, if you'll just hand me that form there, I can put it here on my desk to do after I get back from goin' to eat."

Joseph nodded his head. "Okay." Motioning to the blood donation box on the floor, he added: "what do you want me to do with this?"

The woman blushed a little bit, embarrassed to have forgotten about the actual blood being donated. "Oops. I knew I was forgettin' somethin'." She stood up from her desk and walked over to stand next to Joseph. "I've never been all that strong, but maybe you can help me carry this around back?" Suzanne motioned with her arm to a set of swinging doors off to the left.

"Sure thing," Joseph agreed. He liked that arrangement better, anyway. He hadn't been happy about just leaving his precious virus sitting out in the reception area in that sketch part of New York. Joseph felt his back muscles strain as he bent over and picked up the heavy box. *Uhhh*, he grunted. *I'm getting too old for this.*

"Thanks hun'," Suzanne said with a smile. "You're such a help."

Again with the 'hun,' Joseph thought. *Whatever. As long as she doesn't start asking more questions. This lady looks like she'd win Gossip of the Year at her church.*

Putting his last set of twelve blood pints down just behind the swinging doors that lead to what Joseph assumed was the actual blood storage area, the doctor stood up and wiped his hands together, symbolically cleaning them of what had been his life's work for the past two years. "Anything else I need to do?"

"Nope, I think you're all set. Let's get out of here so we can both go get some food."

"Sounds good to me," Joseph answered truthfully. He was starting to get hungry. Shaking the older woman's hand for good measure, the domestic terrorist breathed a deep sigh of relief as he turned and exited the Red Cross donation center. *It's done.*

****

About an hour and half after the slender, gray-haired man left, after Suzanne had taken her lunch break at the Chick-fil-A down the street, the grandmother of five sat down at her desk to enter the information on Joseph's donation form into her computer. She didn't like technology, had a tendency to put what should be personal messages as publicly available Facebook status updates, and still occasionally forgot that she needed to put spaces between the words on her text messages. Nonetheless, after three years at the Red Cross, Suzanne could finally manage to do her required work without too many computer errors.

Still pecking at the keyboard with her two index fingers, the receptionist began to type.

Name: Jim Finch. She had never heard of or met the man before, but Suzanne realized that she didn't know everyone involved in the local Red Cross. She knew most of the regulars, but this Mr. Finch must have just been able to help today for the first time.

Address: 351 Cumberland Hills Drive. *Hmm, that's weird*, Suzanne thought. When she entered the given street name and number into her computer, it popped up on the screen as the home address of Alex and Melanie Kuzio, two of northern Nashville's most active blood donors. The kind of people who marked their calendars to give blood every eight weeks – as often as they were allowed.

"Hey Max?" the receptionist called out, trying to get the attention of her boss. When the man didn't answer, she tried again more loudly: "Max!"

Suzanne heard footsteps approaching and then saw the swinging doors open. "What is it?" the man ten years her junior asked. Max had been with the Red Cross ever since he retired from the Air Force twenty years earlier, but he had only recently moved to the Nashville area from San Diego.

"I'm putting in the information for that blood donation we got earlier," the receptionist began, "and the address that the man gave me comes back as being the same as Alex and Melanie Kuzio, who are two of our most frequent donors."

Max picked up the form and looked at Joseph's scribbled handwriting. "So it is a valid address?" he asked.

When Suzanne nodded her head affirmatively, Max surmised: "maybe he just wrote it wrong. Or maybe that other couple moved." He put the paper back down on Suzanne's desk, not appearing worried at all. "I'm sure it's fine." The office manager wanted to add that all of the paperwork didn't really matter, that no one ever actually did anything with it, but he caught himself before he did since he knew that his friendly receptionist would feel bad about her work being labeled as not important. Taking a deep breath, Max added: "I appreciate you double checking with me, though. That's good work to stay on top of things. We're lucky to have you, Suzanne."

The blonde woman smiled, bleached white teeth on full display. Her boss' attempt at flattery had clearly worked. "Thanks so much. You're such a sweetheart. And you're right, I'm sure the address thing is fine."

****

After Joseph's third and final long drive home, back in his suburban neighborhood, on a street still lined with sparkly pink ribbons and signs about the missing Peyton Finch, the middle-aged bachelor sat on the leather couch in his living room and released a deep sigh of contentment. Finally finished with his two-year long project, Joseph had poured himself a glass of scotch and was now slowly sipping it in between puffs on his Cuban cigar. It was a Romeo y Julieta, his favorite kind. An acquaintance of Joseph's from medical school now lived and worked in Europe, and, knowing his former classmate's affinity for the embargoed cigars, always bought Joseph a box whenever he went to Cuba on business.

Joseph liked the smell and the taste of the Romeo y Julieta, and he liked the story behind its name as well. The cigars were hand-rolled in large factories, and the women who worked there were read books over a loudspeaker to pass the time. The cigar names matched the story titles. 'Romeo y Julieta.' 'Montecristo.' Etcetera. Much like Winston Churchill and countless others before him, Joseph was a Romeo y Julieta devotee.

Joseph released a long, deep sigh. He couldn't believe it was all finally over. The hours upon hours of work. The literal blood and sweat he had invested in the project. Although no tears . . . Joseph didn't do tears.

Yes, it was finally over. And yet, in a way, Operation Respect was just beginning. The virus was now in play, and whether it succeeded or failed was completely out of Joseph's hands. All he could do now was sit back, smoke a cigar, drink his scotch, and wait.

PART II: THE TASK FORCE

TWELVE

"We have an outbreak on our hands, Mr. President."

The White House Deputy Chief of Staff and seasoned political advisor pulled no punches in his description of the situation, not phased at all by his Oval Office surroundings or the world's most powerful man seated behind the desk in front of him.

"This isn't an outbreak," another senior staffer responded. "Six cases in random parts of the country is not an outbreak. More people were probably infected with HIV having sex last night in DC alone."

President Hughes listened as two of his top advisors argued in front of him during their daily early morning staff meeting. "First of all," he finally replied, pointing to the second advisor, "can we not start our morning by talking about the sexual habits of the population of Washington, DC., please? Secondly, as you said yourself, Caroline, when we heard about the third case, this is not just some randoms being infected with a virus. This is people checking into very reputable hospitals for completely unrelated surgeries or treatments, seemingly fine when they leave, but then coming down with a sickness that resembles AIDS and dying within a couple of weeks. So instead of standing there arguing about semantics, whether or not this qualifies as an 'outbreak,' why don't you tell me what we're going to do to solve this."

"Yes, Mr. President," his Chief of Staff, Daniel Bader, responded. "We were initially notified of the situation by the Centers for Disease Control in Atlanta, and they've sent people to each hospital involved to collect information about all of the suspected cases. We're also considering bringing in another pathologist to try to find out how this is happening."

"Stop considering and do it," the president ordered.
"Who?"
"I beg your pardon, sir?"
"You must have someone in mind. Some doctor to head the investigation."
"Well, Mr. President," his Deputy Chief of Staff chimed in, "Isaac Carlson is the best pathologist, but –"
"No buts. I want him on this. Now."
The deputy spoke up again. "Sir, Dr. Carlson has a full load of patients and cases and research –"
"He works out of a National Institute of Health lab, isn't that right?" Daniel Bader asked.
"Well, yeah . . ."
"Then he works for us," the Chief of Staff concluded.
President Hughes nodded his head in agreement. "Exactly. If he's good enough for government funding, then he's good enough for government work. Hell, conscript him if you have to. But I want Carlson in charge of the investigation. And a team of the best from NIH and the CDC assisting him. Understood?"
The two men and one woman across from the president's desk nodded in acquiescence to his orders. The fourth staffer in the room, the Communications Director, then spoke for the first time. "Mr. President, what do you want me to do about the press?"
Daniel Bader responded on behalf of his boss. "Don't hide anything. If they ask a question, answer it. But don't volunteer any information either."
When his staff didn't respond to their latest instructions, Richard Hughes expressed his frustration. "What are you still standing here for? Go to work."

****

It's amazing how quickly the government can mobilize something into action when it really wants to, Keri Dupree thought as she found herself seated at a large oval table in the middle of Conference Room D at the National Institutes of Health. Less than twenty-four hours ago, Dr. Dupree, a noted pathologist, had been working with her boss, Isaac Carlson – an even more noted pathologist – on a way to incorporate more than the usual three virus strands into the annual flu vaccine. But now, on this bright, mid-April Thursday morning, both Keri and Isaac were waiting on their four new colleagues to arrive. Isaac had been asked – well, more like ordered – by the President of the United States to form a task force to combat a mysterious new illness that was killing people around the country. Keri was Isaac's first choice to join him on the project. Having been his Number Two for nearly eight years, there were hardly any cases that Isaac worked on without her.

Although they were less than ten years apart in age – she was thirty-five and he was forty-four – Dr. Carlson had long-since become a sort of father figure to Keri Dupree. They were both doctors, and excellent ones at that, but Dr. Dupree wasn't even in the same stratosphere of renown and talent as her boss, and she knew it. And on the days when she might have been inclined to forget, Isaac had subtle yet forceful ways of reminding her. It wasn't that she thought he was a bad person – he just liked to keep a clearly-defined pecking order in the office. After all, he was double board certified in general surgery and pathology; she was 'merely' a pathologist. He graduated from Harvard Medical School; she went to a state school. He also held a Masters in Public Health from Harvard; she did not. He was the author of numerous books and a member of several national health advisory boards; she was not. But what Keri was, and she knew it, was indispensable to her boss. Isaac Carlson would not be the world-renowned doctor and policy expert that he was without Keri Dupree as his right hand woman. So she put up with his crap, ignored her husband's nearly daily suggestions that she quit, and bided her time until the day arrived when she could finally run her own clinic.

Dr. Dupree softly tapped her nails on the glass covering the mahogany conference room table while they waited on the rest of the task force members to arrive. The two doctors flying up from the Centers for Disease Control in Atlanta were carrying the patient files with them, so all that Keri could do at the moment was sit and wait.

THIRTEEN

Nearly forty-five minutes later, the last members of the task force finally arrived. The first to show had been Dr. Anthony Russo and Dr. Leah Mann, both from the research center at Johns Hopkins University. Anthony was sixty-three and had the dark features one might expect of a person born in Italy. His parents had immigrated to the United States when he was a young boy, with his mom cleaning houses and his dad working in an Italian restaurant until his English improved enough to land a job as a doorman at a building on the Upper East Side. Married for forty-one years to the daughter of other Italian immigrants, Anthony and his wife Angela were the proud parents of five and grandparents of twelve, with the thirteenth already on the way.

Shuffling along beside Dr. Russo was his research assistant, twenty-nine year old Leah Mann. The slightly overweight young woman had shock red hair that looked like it hadn't seen a brush in years and wore not an ounce of makeup, the effect of which was to make her look several years younger than she already was. Leah was biting her nails as she walked into the room, a nervous habit that she knew was unsanitary but had a devil of a time trying to kick. Dr. Mann's baggy jeans, t-shirt, and forgettable face stood out in stark contrast to the debonair Roman man standing next to her.

Keri could already see the irritation in her boss rising when the two immunologists walked in twenty minutes late. Isaac was a perfectionist in every regard – it was one of the things that made him so great at his job, but was simultaneously the reason why he didn't get along well with very many people.

"Hopkins is right down the damn road from here," Isaac had complained before Drs. Mann and Russo arrived. "They should *not* be late."

Her boss did have a point, which Keri quickly acknowledged to keep him from being irritated with her as well. The NIH building where Keri and Isaac worked and where the task force would be meeting was located in Bethesda, Maryland, only a short drive from Baltimore and the Hopkins campus. Nevertheless, it was the first day and traffic in the Washington, DC suburbs was notoriously brutal.

"They'll get here," Keri had assured Isaac. "And we can't do anything until the CDC people arrive anyway."

Dr. Carlson knew she had him beat with that final comment, and had simply nodded his head and returned to pacing the room.

****

Twenty minutes after the Hopkins crew arrived, a taxi dropped off Dr. David Malhotra and Dr. Gill Pingrey at the main entrance to the sprawling National Institutes of Health research facility.

"Nice digs," David said to his travelling partner as they both took a suitcase in one hand and a box of medical files in the other and headed for the entrance. "Thank goodness for automatic doors, huh?" he said light-heartedly, to which Dr. Pingrey issued a short laugh in agreement.

Forty-three year old David Malhotra was definitely one of the big men on campus at the Centers for Disease Control in Atlanta, and not just because of his brilliant work combating infectious diseases. The son of Indian immigrants, David's father was a doctor in his home country but couldn't get licensed in the United States. So he had taken a job as a researcher for a pharmaceutical company and made a comfortable living doing so. Gaurav

Malhotra and his wife had three children, one boy and two girls, who had all gone on to fulfill their parents' American Dream. The older of the two girls was a lawyer, and the youngest child was married to a lawyer. But their first-born and only son, Sahil, had taken on the American name of David and been on the fast-track to success his entire life. He was smart, good-looking, and also just a really nice guy. Dr. Malhotra was known around the CDC for being friendly, easygoing, and always ready with a quick joke or funny story. He was Mr. Congeniality, and the doctor travelling with him was thrilled to have the opportunity to work with David on this task force.

Gill Pingrey was thirty-one, older than Leah Mann but younger than Keri Dupree, and usually focused his research on tropical diseases. But this task force was a career opportunity that he just couldn't pass up. Scion of Atlanta blue bloods, Gill came from the kind of family where his mother and sister were members of both the Daughters of the American Revolution and the Daughters of the Confederacy. His father and older brother worked in finance, and the middle child – given his mother's maiden name – had broken the mold to enter medicine. Dr. Pingrey was still sporting the same floppy hairstyle that he had since his fraternity days at Vanderbilt, and he was engaged to marry his former prep school girlfriend. Despite his background, or perhaps because of it, Gill desperately wanted to prove himself worthy of working on projects like this one. Nonetheless, he wasn't exactly excited about the prospect of daily interaction with Dr. Carlson.

Gill only knew *THE* Isaac Carlson by reputation, but that reputation was one of being arrogant, demanding, and a perfectionist. Although, interestingly enough, Gill had run across a website during the flight up from Atlanta that morning which was created by a former patient of Dr. Carlson. It was full of testimonials about how nice Isaac had been and how he would seemingly become an extension of the patients' families while he was treating them. *Maybe he's just a jerk to the people he works with,* Gill thought, pressing 'three' on the elevator buttons and bracing himself as the floor beneath him began to rise. *Either way it doesn't bode well for me.*

****

"Alright, let's introduce ourselves," Isaac said, wanting to waste no time. Drs. Malhotra and Pingrey had just deposited their luggage in the corner of the large room and set the patient file boxes on top of the table, and the two men were now seated directly across from Isaac and Keri. Dr. Russo was in a chair next to the two CDC doctors and Leah Mann, clearly seeking some sort of comfort in a room full of men, had taken her spot next to Keri – the only other woman in the group.

I can see why this girl went into research, Keri thought. Obviously Leah was smart; she wouldn't be on the task force if she wasn't. *She just looks like she could use a little work on her social skills. And a makeover,* Keri mentally added. *Definitely a makeover.*

"I'll start," Dr. Carlson declared, pulling his associate's attention away from the meek young woman on her left to the always confident, highly accomplished man on her right. "I've met some of you before but for those I haven't, I'm Isaac Carlson. I'm Chief of Pathology here at the NIH." The skinny, gray-haired man had the full attention of the room as he spoke. He usually had that effect on people. Something about his calm but strong tone of voice and his confident mannerisms conveyed that he was a man of intellect and power and should be listened to. Isaac Carlson wasn't really as powerful as his speech portrayed (especially outside of his chosen field of medicine), but he was definitely brilliant and definitely the one in charge of the meeting taking place in Conference Room D.

"I was asked by the White House," Isaac went on, "to put together a task force and tackle the mysterious illness that has claimed six lives so far. Obviously," he said as he gestured around the room, "since you're here, you're on the team. For the heck of it, since we will be working together a lot for the foreseeable future, I grew up in Seattle, went to Harvard Medical School, and my favorite color is green."

The other doctors in the room snickered a little bit at Isaac's last line. His gray-blue eyes shone briefly behind his always-present glasses. The meeting was off to a good start.

"Keri, why don't you go next," the group's captain suggested.

Keri Dupree nodded her head in agreement, her brown, shoulder-length hair bouncing slightly as she did. The movement easily caught the attention of the three men sitting across the table from her. Or maybe it was her deep, chocolate-colored eyes. Or, perhaps, the way her specially tailored lab coat clung just enough in all the right places. Beside Keri, Leah Mann sighed as she saw the appreciative looks on the other doctors' faces. *No one ever looks at me that way.*

Dr. Dupree, oblivious as to her effect on the room, smiled and made a specialized effort to make eye contact with each of her new colleagues. Her husband, a successful trial lawyer, had taught her about the importance of making eye contact with her audience. For him, the audience was the jury. For Keri, it was the four fresh faces in this conference room. Keri wasn't much concerned about making eye contact with Isaac. He knew her well enough already.

"Okay," she finally said, "I'm Dr. Keri Dupree. I also work here at the NIH in Isaac's lab. I'm originally from

Fort Wayne, Indiana, I went to the University of Pittsburgh for medical school, and my favorite color is yellow."

"Yellow?" Isaac asked disapprovingly. "No one's favorite color is yellow."

"Well it's mine," Keri answered haughtily. She was in too good of a mood and too excited about this new task force to let her boss' often grumpy personality bother her today.

Seizing control of the situation, Dr. Dupree turned slightly in her chair to face the young doctor beside her. The slightly chubby redhead jumped when Keri placed her hand on the girl's forearm, but she didn't shy away as the older of the two said: "you're next, honey." The 'honey' at the end wasn't meant to be derogatory or condescending, but as soon as the word left Keri's lips she worried that the men in the room had taken it the wrong way. All she wanted to do was signal to the obviously skittish young woman that it was okay to come out of her shell a little bit.

Leah Mann didn't seem to be bothered in the least by Keri's comment. She picked at the corner of a piece of paper in front of her as she began to speak, looking at the paper more often than she did the other people in the room.

"Umm . . . hi," she said quietly. "My name is Leah Mann. It's spelled like one syllable, 'lee,' but pronounced with two syllables, 'lee-uh.' I'm twenty-nine. I went to Hopkins for undergrad and medical school." Thankfully, Keri noted, no one said anything as the youngest of the group gave much more background information than was required. "I'm originally from Milwaukee, Wisconsin," Dr. Mann continued, "and I don't really have a favorite color." Leah paused. "Although I do like yellow," she added, smiling slightly at Dr. Dupree. "Yellow is pretty."

"See!" Keri declared triumphantly, aiming her gloating in the direction of her boss. "Leah likes yellow too."

"Whatever," Isaac sighed, shaking his head before fixing his attention across the table. "Dr. Russo, your favorite color isn't yellow as well, is it?"

The heavyset but well-composed sixty-three year old laughed in response. "No, it's not. My favorite color is red." In spite of the fact that he was born in Italy, Anthony's voice carried no trace of an Italian accent. Anthony had been in the medical business for longer than several of his new colleagues had been alive, giving him the kind of gravitas that only came with experience.

"Like Isaac just said, I'm Dr. Russo. Anthony Russo," he elaborated. "I work and teach at Johns Hopkins. Leah here is my best research assistant." Anthony paused long enough to see his young prodigy smile and blush at the compliment, then continued introducing himself. "I went to Columbia Medical School a long, long time ago. And although I feel like a New Yorker, my dear mama – may she rest in peace," he inserted, crossing himself as he did – "would come up from her grave and haunt me if I didn't say I was from Italy."

His comments drew gentle laughter from the group, and once again Isaac remarked to himself how well the meeting appeared to be going. *I picked a good group*, he thought proudly.

The next person to speak occupied the center seat in his row, directly across from Keri.

"Hey y'all," was the dark-haired, dark-skinned man's opening line, and Isaac couldn't help but grin a little bit at the obvious contrast between the man's ethnic appearance and his good ol' boy Southern accent. "I'm David Malhotra. I'm head of the Division of High-Consequence Pathogens and Pathology at the CDC."

"Why does the federal government think every office needs twelve names?" Isaac interrupted. "It's like when you read the full names of kings and queens. George William James Joseph John Phillip . . . nobody needs that many names. There's your sign that the government is too big – it has so many offices that each one has to have fifteen-word titles just to be able to tell them all apart."

Leah leaned over to the brunette doctor sitting next to her, the one who had introduced herself as Keri Dupree. In a hushed voice she asked, "he does realize that his office is funded by the federal government, right?"

Keri gave a half-smile and a sigh in response. "He does," she whispered back. "Just ignore his little rants. You'll get used to them."

When Isaac had finished with his soliloquy, David Malhotra took it all in stride and continued: "I was born and raised in the Atlanta area, I went to Duke for med school, and my favorite color is blue. Navy blue, if we're getting picky about it."

David's introduction was short, sweet, and to the point, and all of the other doctors in the room immediately liked him. One doesn't go to Duke Med or rise to the top spot of the CDC's infectious disease unit without being brilliant, but unlike the other brilliant man at the table (the notoriously demanding leader of the task force), this Dr. Malhotra guy appeared to be a genuinely friendly and engaging person.

****

I was wrong, Isaac thought as the sixth and final task force member began to introduce himself. *David Malhotra doesn't have a good ol' boy accent. This kid has a good ol' boy accent. Holy crap. I almost need a translator.*

The voice with the accent belonged to Dr. Gill Pingrey, the Atlanta native with light brown hair and ice blue eyes who was dressed like he belonged in a J.Crew catalog and had just finished telling the group that he went to Emory Medical School. "I also got my Masters in Biomedical Engineering at Oxford in between college and med school."

"Rhodes Scholar?" Anthony guessed.

"Yep," Gill confirmed with a nod. "I work at the CDC with David in the DHCPP," the young man continued, "and my favorite color is also blue. Although I'm more partial to a royal blue," he smiled.

"You two can compare paint samples later," Isaac remarked half-jokingly. "Now what do you say we get going with the patient files? How did this whole thing get started anyway?"

FOURTEEN

"How are you feeling, Grandma?" The concerned voice of her youngest granddaughter woke Edna Jenkins from the daydream she had been having, one in which she was a young girl again, dancing with her high school sweetheart at the county fair. "Grandma?" the voice asked again.

"I hear you, don't worry. I'm not dead yet." Edna could hear the exacerbated sighs of the people in the room as she made light of her near-death experience in a car crash the day before. Edna liked to crack jokes about her age . . . she figured if she had lived this long, to the ripe old age of eighty-three, she was entitled to do and say pretty much whatever she wanted to. Her favorite was to purposely call people by the wrong name to make them think she was losing her memory. Worked every time.

But today Edna could tell that her family's worrying was different. They weren't just concerned because she was old; they were concerned because she had been in a pretty bad accident. The doctors told her yesterday after she woke up from surgery that she had broken two ribs and a compound fracture on her left arm, and that they had to use a steel plate and screws to fix all of it. *When you add in my dentures and the new hip I got several years back, I practically have a whole hardware store inside my body now*, Edna thought with dismay.

"Will one of you hand me my eyes so I can see you?" she asked. Edna already had a pretty good idea of who would be in the room, and putting on her glasses confirmed it. Her only child, a son named Wade, was standing right beside her bed, looking stern and serious as usual. Edna knew he couldn't help it . . . Wade looked just like his daddy. Edna's late husband wasn't the boy she had been dancing with in her daydream. Her husband, Wade Sr., didn't like to dance. The boy from the daydream was Billy, and he used to light up a dance floor like Fred Astaire. Billy had shipped out to Korea for the 'police action' there, and Edna promised to wait for him. When he came back in a casket, Edna was devastated. And the Jenkins boy was there. So she married solid, dependable, serious-looking Wade Sr., built a good home, raised a good son, and dreamed about her dances with Billy.

Wade Jr.'s wife, Sally, was also in the room, along with the younger of their two daughters. Vanessa was twenty-five and taught fourth grade at a local elementary school. The older daughter, Jenny, had left their small Colorado town for Los Angeles as soon as she could and hadn't looked back. Jenny had dreams of being a model or actress, but like many before her had settled for life as a clerk in a doctor's office.

Boy, these three sure look worried, Edna thought as she surveyed her family standing before her. She was worried too, but for different reasons. Wade Sr. had passed away five years ago and, up until now, Edna had continued to live by herself, but she knew this wreck would change things. She had been on her way to the grocery store when she came up on an intersection. Edna meant to hit the brake, but she punched the gas pedal instead and slammed into the back of the car in front of her. *Something like this was just what Wade Jr. and Sally needed to finally get their way and make me move in with them*, Edna thought. *They'll take away my car keys, my driver's license, my house . . .* a trickle of tears began to fill the elderly woman's eyes as she realized that this wreck meant the loss of her independence and the life she had built for herself. *They'll take away my freedom.*

"Momma, are you alright? You're crying," her son noticed. "Vanessa, go get the nurse," Wade commanded.

"No, no, I'm fine. I'm fine. No need to bother anybody," Edna replied. "And as soon as the doctors release me, I won't be a bother to you all anymore either. I'll just take myself on home." Edna figured it was at least worth a shot, right?

****

Wrong. Edna hadn't just taken herself on home. Instead, things went exactly as she predicted. Wade and Sally were adamant that she couldn't go home by herself, and the doctor agreed that she needed help until her broken bones fully healed. But Edna knew better. This wasn't merely a temporary stay. This was permanent. *I've now become that little old lady who can't take care of herself. A burden to her family*, Edna thought miserably.

"They may make me leave my house and move in here, but they can't make me be happy about it," Edna declared to an empty bedroom in the basement of her son and daughter-in-law's house. "And we really need to do something about these living quarters." Edna had spent five days in the hospital recovering from the wreck and surgery, and this morning – after her first night's sleep at Wade's house – she had woken up with a nasty cough that hadn't gotten any better as the day progressed. It was now late afternoon and she still didn't feel all that well, but that was probably just her body's reaction to the painkillers she was taking. "If they're going to stick me down here in this dungeon the least they could do is give me a dehumidifier or something," the elderly woman grumbled as she and her walker slowly rolled their way across the carpet to the bathroom.

A knock on the bedroom door interrupted Edna's use of the facilities. "Edna? Are you in there?" asked Sally. "I just wanted to let you know that I'm home from work and wanted to see how you're doing."

"Just a minute," Edna replied. "Hold your horses." Edna knew she sounded irritated and that later that night

Sally would once again ask Wade why his mother hated her, but the truth was that she didn't hate her daughter-in-law. Sure, Edna wasn't happy about having to move in here, even temporarily as they claimed. But right now she was more irritated by her cough and the fact that the wheels on her walker kept getting stuck in the grooves of the carpet. Exasperated and exhausted, Edna finally gave up. "It's unlocked, Sally. You might as well let yourself in. I'll turn one hundred before I make it all the way over to the door."

Sally Jenkins slowly opened the door to the spare bedroom that now housed her mother-in-law. Sally had always gotten the impression that Edna didn't approve of her, and if the older woman's tone of voice right now was any indication, today had another lecture or scolding in store.

The preemptive scowl on Sally's face quickly turned to a worried frown when she got her first glimpse of Edna. Her mother-in-law had seemed fine when Sally and Wade left for work that morning, but now she looked tired and extremely pale. To top it all off, the elder Mrs. Jenkins issued a thunderous, hacking cough that turned to wheezing at the end as she struggled for air.

"Edna!" Sally exclaimed worriedly. "Here, sit down on the bed. I'll get you some water." As Sally quickly returned from the bathroom sink with a full glass in her hand, her eyes surveyed over the new houseguest. Edna really didn't look well. At all. Handing the water to the other woman, Sally asked: "how long have you had this cough? Is anything else bothering you?"

"Oh, I'm fine. Quit your worrying," came Edna's reply. "I woke up with the cough this morning, but it's probably just this damp basement."

Sally deliberately ignored the comment about the inadequacy of her house and continued, "you look pale too."

"Probably because I just had to do the old lady shuffle all the way over to the bathroom and back." Edna's argument was interrupted by the sound of a car door slamming shut outside.

"That's Wade. I'm bringing him down here."

****

Sally returned a few moments later with her husband. "See, honey, she really doesn't look good."

"Don't you know that's not something you're supposed to say to a woman?" Edna bit out, sarcasm mixing with irritation in her voice.

"This isn't a time for jokes, Momma," Wade replied. "Sally says you've had a bad cough all day."

"Which will go away if you put a dehumidifier down here."

Wade ignored his mother's response and stepped in front of where she was sitting on the bed. He placed his hand on her forehead to check for a fever and quickly jerked his arm backward. "Mom! You're burning up!"

Sally repeated the test and also pulled her hand away from the scalding forehead. "That settles it. Wade, you stay here with your mom. I'm going to call her doctor."

FIFTEEN

"Tell me about the first patient," Isaac asked the doctor seated across the conference table from him. David Malhotra's Centers for Disease Control in Atlanta usually handled strange outbreaks like this – they even had David's special, long-named unit for it, the Infectious Diseases Pathology Branch of the Division of High-Consequence Pathogens and Pathology – but Isaac had been chosen personally by the President to head this task force . . . something that made him swell with pride but undoubtedly angered his CDC counterparts. And because Dr. Carlson was Dr. Carlson, he felt a need to definitively take charge of this and all future meetings with his task force colleagues.

Taking a manila envelope from the top of the stack in front of him, Dr. Malhotra opened the case file. "The first patient who was documented as presenting with these symptoms was an eighty-three year old woman from Colorado."

"What's her name?" Isaac asked.

"Uhh . . ." David stalled, looking for the answer. "Edna Jenkins."

"I find that I work better when I can attach a name and a face to the case," Isaac clarified.

"Okay, whatever," the CDC expert said dismissively. "Anyway, the patient – Edna Jenkins – came in to the hospital with fatigue, a persistent cough, and a 102-degree fever. Doctors there were able to get the fever down, but the cough continued and then a rash and sore throat appeared. Mrs. Jenkins also complained of severe joint pain, although there's a note here that the joint pain could have been caused by the car wreck that she was in a week earlier."

"Wait, so let's get the timeline straight," said Dr. Carlson. "Edna is in a wreck, and then a week later she shows up at the hospital with those symptoms?"

"Actually, no, I skipped some stuff," David replied, a little too flippantly for Isaac's liking.

"You skipped some stuff? 'Skipped some stuff'? Let me clarify something here, people," Isaac said, looking around the room at the team of highly regarded pathologists. "There is a disease spreading in this country and we don't know what it is, where it's headed, or how to stop it. Now the President of the United States has tasked us with solving this before we have a public panic on our hands. So we will not skip any stuff. We will learn our patients' names. And we will work around the clock until we figure this out and beat this thing. Understood?"

Ten pairs of eyes slowly nodded up and down as Dr. Carlson's team responded to his speech.

"Alright then. David, once more, and from the beginning this time, tell me about the first patient."

****

"I'm sorry to have to bring this up, Mr. Jenkins, but has your mother discussed her end of life plans with you?"

Wade's first instinct was to be furious at the young medical intern's question. *End of life? We're not at that point yet.* But, in the next instant, he realized that it was a valid question. And they were at that point.

His mother had been admitted to the hospital a week ago, the same day that he and his wife had come home from work to find her sick. Edna's doctor said it probably wasn't anything serious, but given her age and the trauma her body had recently gone through he wanted to be extra cautious. The medical team at the hospital had been able to make the fever go away, but his mom still wouldn't stop coughing – so much so that it irritated her airway and she started coughing up blood.

Four days into her hospital stay, the doctors still had no idea what was wrong. They would get one symptom under control only to have another one start. To Wade, it seemed like some sort of disease whack-a-mole. On the fourth day at the hospital, though, things changed. The whack-a-mole game went into hyper-drive. Edna got a splitting headache, then diarrhea, and then little white lesions started showing up on the inside of her mouth. Wade's mother had been unconscious since that afternoon three days ago.

A doctor, the same one who was still waiting for an answer about Edna's end of life plans, had suggested testing the elderly patient for AIDS. All of the symptoms were the same, he said. They were just coming in rapid succession, whereas AIDS is a very slowly developing disease. Wade had yelled at the doctors; told them it was absolutely ridiculous to even suggest that his mother would have a disease like AIDS. The hospital did the test anyway, probably because they had already run out of other ideas. And it came back negative, just like Wade said it would.

"Mr. Jenkins? Did you hear me?" the doctor repeated.

"What? Yeah, I heard you. She's got a cemetery plot next to my dad, but we never talked about a living will or anything like that."

"That's okay. A lot of people don't. I'm going to send our hospital's end of life specialist up here to talk with you, just in case. As Mrs. Jenkins is a widow and you're her only son, decisions will fall to you as next of kin."

Wade simply nodded his head in response. Next of kin. The words raced through his mind. *I can't be making decisions like that. Come on, Momma. Wake up,* Wade silently pleaded as he knelt down beside his mother's hospital bed. *Wake up and beat this thing.*

****

"Mrs. Jenkins died eight days after being admitted to the hospital for the fever and cough. Doctors there listed her cause of death as unknown," Dr. Malhotra concluded as he finished his renewed description of the task force's first patient.

"Please tell me they haven't buried her yet. Or that they at least collected samples before turning her over to the family." The last thing Isaac wanted was to have to fly out to Colorado to exhume somebody's dead grandmother.

"They got samples," David replied. "Blood, urine, stool, saliva, hair, and skin."

"Good," Dr. Carlson nodded his head approvingly. "That will make our job a lot easier." Placing his hands down on the mahogany table and slowly standing up, Isaac announced: "let's take a quick break to grab some lunch from the cafeteria downstairs. Bring the food back up here, though. We'll be working while we eat."

SIXTEEN

"Okay people, let's get started. Who has the file on the second patient?" Isaac asked in between forkfuls of salad. The cafeteria at the NIH building certainly wasn't award-winning, but it wasn't terrible either.

"I have that one as well," David answered, putting down the sandwich he had brought with him that day and picking up another manila folder. "The second suspected case of whatever it is we're dealing with was out of Texas. A seventeen year old girl named Taylor Stone who was being treated in Houston for leukemia."

"Before you go any further, David," Isaac interrupted. "What's your name again? Yeah, you in the red shirt," he asked as he leaned forward and pointed at the woman two seats down from him. In between the two people, Keri shook her head. She knew that Isaac remembered the other woman's name; the man had a mind like a sponge . . . he remembered everything. Isaac just wanted to give off the impression that the girl on Keri's left wasn't yet important enough for him to remember.

Leah looked surprised to be singled out in the conversation. "Umm, it's Leah. I'm Dr. Leah Mann."

"Right. Okay, Dr. Mann, why don't you go over to that whiteboard against the wall and keep track of everything these patients have in common. Make us a little chart or something."

After Leah had taken up her post by the whiteboard, dry-erase marker in hand, David continued with reading the file. "Okay, patient number two. Female, seventeen, in the hospital undergoing chemotherapy for Stage Three leukemia. Taylor, this girl, had seemingly beaten the cancer when she was fourteen but it came back. She was five weeks into the chemo when she started having unexplained symptoms."

"How did hers start?" Keri asked.

****

"Hey, Jodie, can I ask you something?" Taylor Stone said quietly, not wanting to worry her nurse or alert her parents who were standing just outside in the hospital hallway.

"Sure, honey. What is it?" Jodie LeClair asked as she hung a fresh bag of chemotherapy drugs on her young patient's IV pole. Jodie had also worked with Taylor during the girl's first bout with leukemia three years ago and had gotten to know her well.

"It's probably nothing," Taylor began hesitantly, "but I've had a really bad sore throat for like a whole day, and now I have this pounding headache," the girl added, bringing her free hand up to touch by her temple.

Taylor's mention of new symptoms immediately got Jodie's attention, mainly because the young woman usually never complained about anything. "How long have you had the headache?" the nurse asked.

"I dunno. A couple of hours maybe?"

"Why didn't you say something sooner, sweetie?" Jodie said, trying to mask the scolding tone rising in her voice.

Taylor responded by shrugging her shoulders. "I didn't want to bother anybody."

"Oh Taylor . . ." Nurse LeClair sighed as she turned and headed out of the teenager's room to find the attending physician. Chemotherapy definitely produced side effects, but a sore throat and a headache weren't usually among them. And Taylor had never had that kind of reaction before to her treatment. Something wasn't right.

As soon as the nurse exited the room, Taylor knew she shouldn't have said anything to her about the sore throat and the headache. A really cute boy from her school, one she had been crushing on hard for the past several months, had sent her a Facebook message last night saying that he was going to stop by the hospital after school today to see her. But he couldn't come now. Immediately after Taylor's doctor heard about her new symptoms, he made her move from her regular hospital room into a weird quarantine area. Only doctors and nurses were allowed in her room now, and they had to wear special scrubs and masks when they did come inside. Even her parents and her younger brother had to talk to her through a microphone buzzer thing in the wall. *All because of a stupid headache*, Taylor thought. *Okay, so maybe it's not just a headache. My throat hurts and I feel nauseous and my whole body is starting to feel like it's being pressed down into the bed by a human-sized panini maker.*

Alarms sounding from the machines next to her bed made Taylor jump with surprise and sent her medical team rushing in. Taylor's eyes then suddenly became very heavy, and the voices of the doctors kept getting farther and farther away . . .

****

"Okay, Leah. Recap for us. What does Taylor Stone have in common with Edna Jenkins?" Isaac asked. His team had now finished their lunches – except for Dr. Mann, of course, who had been busy filling in the whiteboard as David read through Patient Number Two's file.

"Well," she began, "they're both female. Both Caucasian. They were both patients in the hospital either at the point when the symptoms showed up or just prior to it. The initial symptoms were different. For number one –"

"Names, Dr. Mann," Isaac chided.

"Right, sorry. Edna Jenkins' first symptom was a cough, then fatigue and a fever. Taylor Stone had a sore throat and a headache. The fever that put Taylor in a coma didn't show up until at least twenty-four hours after the sore throat."

"Okay, what else?" Dr. Carlson asked.

"The mouth sores," Gill replied, answering the question before his counterpart had a chance to. "Both Edna and Taylor had white sores on the inside of their mouths a few days in." He paused. "And they both died."

Isaac pursed his lips together and briefly nodded his head, a sign that his task force colleagues were quickly discovering meant that their boss wasn't happy about whatever the person just said. This time, Isaac was upset because he didn't like it when his patients died. It meant he had failed.

SEVENTEEN

"Patient three, let's hear it," Isaac stated.

This time it wasn't David who reached for a folder. Instead, Isaac's extremely competent assistant, Dr. Keri Dupree, picked up a file in front of her. "Thomas George. Also from Texas."

"Houston?" Leah asked, drawing a line down the whiteboard to create another column.

"No," the thirty-five year old brunette answered. "This one is from the panhandle, up near Lubbock." Keri looked back down at the case file in front of her. "Mr. George was forty-eight. Lived and worked on a cattle ranch."

"Do we think it might be regional?" Isaac asked. He had been trying, from the beginning, to see connections between these patients – aside from their symptoms, of course. It all had to connect somehow. "We've got a Colorado and two from Texas," he added. "Leah, make another column for possible connections and put region or geography up there."

Dr. Mann nodded her head and followed the task force director's instructions.

"I'm sorry, Keri," Isaac said. "Keep going."

****

"Honey, will you come look at this?" Thomas George called to his wife, Marion. The tall, freckled, red-headed Texan was in their bedroom closet putting on his jeans and pullover fleece, getting ready to head out for another day of work on his cattle ranch.

"Did you say something?" Marion asked as she walked into the bedroom. The homely brunette had just finished getting their thirteen-year-old twins on the bus for school.

"Yeah, come look at this," Thomas repeated. He pulled his jeans back down and pointed to a swollen, red circle on the middle of his left thigh.

"Eww, what is that?" his wife asked.

"I dunno. That's why I asked you."

"Does it hurt?" she responded, lightly touching on the irritated spot.

"Like the dickens. And the pressure from my pants rubbing against it is hell. Plus it's hot, do you feel that?"

"Mmmhmm," agreed Marion, scrunching up her nose and eyebrows in a way that her husband of fifteen years knew was her concentrating face. "Did you get bit by something?"

Shaking his head no, Thomas answered: "not that I know of."

"Strange," Marion said, still exhibiting her concentrating look. "Well, let's just put some medicine on it and see if it gets better. And if that doesn't work then you might have to go see the doctor."

"About a little red spot?" Thomas scoffed. "I'm not paying $30 for an office visit so the doc can tell me I got bit by a bug and to put some ointment on it."

****

"How's that red spot, Tom?" Marion asked a few days later. She knew she would have to keep asking him about it, even to the point of making a doctor appointment, for her husband to ever get better. *No wonder men who are married live longer . . . they have a wife to take care of them*, Marion thought.

"Still there," her husband answered. Thomas knew he should probably go see somebody about the spot, especially since it was now nearly sand dollar size and had grown hard and rough to the touch.

"You need to go to the doctor about it," Marion chided. "Especially if it's getting worse."

"I know, I know. Things are just so busy right now."

Marion gave her husband the same I'm-calling-you-on-your-excuses face that she often aimed at their children. "I'm making an appointment for you. And you're going."

Thomas sighed. "I don't get to eat dinner until I agree to this, do I?" he asked. When his wife shook her head no, he finally caved. "Alright, fine. I'll go."

****

"You have what?" Marion asked. Her husband had just left the doctor's office after finally visiting him about the spot on his leg and was now talking to her on his cell phone.

"It's called MRSA. M-R-S-A. Meth resistant stap-lair, or however you pronounce the big name," he answered. "It's some sort of infection."

"How do we fix that? Take some pills or something?" Thomas could hear the worry in Marion's voice as she spoke, but he also couldn't help but smile a little at his wife's use of 'we.' In Marion's mind, Thomas didn't have an infection; they both did.

"Yeah," the rancher replied, "but the doc said he has to wait until the tests come back so he can know what kind of antibiotics to give me."

"Oh, okay," Marion said distractedly as her thumb quickly scrolled through the Wikipedia page she had pulled up on her phone about the infection. "So are you on your way home now?"

Thomas sighed. "No. I've gotta go over to the hospital now so they can drain all of the puss and crap out of the red spot. Doc said I might have to get some new blood too since I've had that spot for so long and it ain't any better."

"Thomas Ryan George!" Marion yelled. She had just finished reading the MRSA description online, and the worry she was feeling came across as anger when she spoke. "I *told* you to go to the doctor sooner!"

"Oh calm down, woman," Thomas replied as he flipped on his blinker and waited to turn into the hospital parking lot. "I'll be fine. Hospitals do blood transfusions all the time. We'll get the spot drained out, doc will give me some drugs, and I'll be fixed in no time."

****

"Mr. George was undergoing treatment for a mild case of MRSA when his symptoms began to appear," Keri read aloud from the folder on the table in front of her. "We don't have all that great of a file on him because he didn't go to the hospital until he was in the very late stages."

"Why not?" Anthony asked.

"Apparently he thought his symptoms were just related to the MRSA," Dr. Dupree answered. "By the time he did finally make it to the emergency room, his wife said he had been complaining of a cough, fatigue, and a rash for a week."

"Wait," Leah broke in. "Could this just be a bad outbreak of MRSA? Maybe a new strand? The symptoms are all fairly similar."

Isaac gave a look of disapproval to his young colleague, who was standing at the whiteboard looking quite proud of herself. "Leah, you will learn as you progress in your career that 'fairly similar' and 'the same' are two entirely different things."

"She's got a point, though, Isaac," Dr. Malhotra chimed in.

Isaac acknowledged that fact by nodding his head. "Gill," he said in reference to David's colleague from the CDC who as yet hadn't contributed much to the conversation. "Get on the phone with the hospitals for Edna and Taylor. Ask them to check the samples for a staph infection." As Gill got up from the table and left the room to make his phone calls, Isaac added, "but it's not staph. Mark my words."

"Okay, well, regardless, let's finish up with Mr. George now," Keri said, trying to get the group back on track. It was one of the things that Isaac appreciated most about his deputy – she always kept everybody in line.

"Yes," Isaac agreed. "We'll finish with Thomas George. But first, before he gets back" – referencing the doctor who had just left the room – "what the hell kind of a name is Gill Pingrey? I mean, seriously."

The rest of the people in the room joined Isaac in snickering at the rather unusual name of one of their fellow task force members. "I think it's a family name," David offered in defense of his friend from the CDC. "He's from an old, Southern family. Gill is probably a mother's maiden name or something like that."

The task force members were clearly unimpressed by Dr. Malhotra's answer, since it ended the fun they were having at the expense of the fratty young member of the group. Keri, however, took the opportunity to restart her description of their patient.

"Like I was saying, regarding the work we're here to do, Mr. George ignored his symptoms for quite a while. His wife said things began to worsen approximately one week after his previous hospital visit, and his health was in steady decline for another week until she finally found him unresponsive in the living room. His fever had spiked, similar to what happened with Taylor Stone, and he never regained consciousness." Keri glanced back down at the file to double check her facts. "Mr. George died forty-eight hours after being admitted to the hospital."

EIGHTEEN

"Let's do one more patient before we call it a day," Isaac suggested. "Who has number four?"

"I do," answered Dr. Pingrey. He had finished calling hospitals about the MRSA tests and was now seated back at the table. "Although, wouldn't it be more accurate to call them victims? I mean, they're all dead."

The majority of the doctors in the room cringed at Gill's comments. He was technically correct, but they also had a pretty good idea how Isaac would respond.

"No, Gill, we will *not* be calling them victims. We are doctors, and they are our patients. If you want to work with victims then I suggest you apply to the police department."

"Okay, sorry," answered a chastised Dr. Pingrey, the color of his cheeks almost matching the red of his tie. Wasting no more time, he opened the file in front of him. "Patient number four is very interesting, actually. Not that the others aren't," Gill quickly added, not wanting to stick his foot in his mouth yet again. Isaac Carlson was one of his idols, the best pathologist in the world, and *here I am, looking like a prize idiot*, Gill thought to himself.

"Are we going to get to hear how he was interesting?" David asked.

"Oh, yeah, sorry," Dr. Pingrey answered hurriedly. "Patient number four is Mr. Andrew Gray. He is thirty years old, or was thirty, and lived in San Francisco."

"And what was his underlying condition?" questioned Isaac.

"I beg your pardon?"

"I think we've established that all of our patients were being treated for something else when their new symptoms appeared. So what did Mr. Gray have?"

"Well," Gill began, "that's the interesting part. He was in the hospital after being attacked on the street, but – and this is what throws me off – he was also HIV positive."

****

"Get a load of this," the emergency room nurse giggled as she leaned over a desk counter to get closer to another trauma nurse working the graveyard shift at San Francisco General Hospital. "You see the guy over there in sick bay three?" she asked, gesturing over her shoulder with her head.

The nurse behind the counter rose up out of her chair and strained her neck to see who her friend and co-worker was talking about. "The one who came in a few minutes ago and who they're prepping for immediate surgery?" she asked, wondering what could be funny about someone is such bad shape.

"Yeah, him," the friend nodded. "I just overheard the police officer who was at the scene talking about it. According to him, the patient tried to rob an old lady down on the Wharf," the first nurse explained, referring to the popular tourist destination on San Francisco's waterfront.

"So how come he's in the hospital?"

"She beat him up!" the nurse exclaimed loudly. When one of the doctors nearby gave her a scolding look, she lowered her voice and then continued: "he walked up to her and told her to hand over her purse. The police officer said that the old lady's response was 'I don't think so, sonny' and then she started whacking him with her cane! Beat the shit out of him too," she concluded, looking over her shoulder as a team of surgery personnel wheeled the badly disfigured man past her and down the hall towards a waiting operating room.

"Good for her," the second nurse declared.

****

"Hold on, was he in the hospital for the street attack or the HIV?" Isaac asked.

"The street attack," Gill replied. "It's protocol at that hospital to run surgical patients' blood for any diseases or infections, and this Andrew Gray showed positive for HIV."

Dr. Russo joined the conversation. "Did he know it beforehand? I mean, given the symptoms, couldn't we be looking at some new mutation of the AIDS virus?"

"None of the other patients so far were HIV positive," David correctly noted.

"Do we know that for sure?" Anthony pressed. His background was in AIDS, since he had been on one of the first teams to investigate it back in the 1980s.

"Yes," came Isaac's confident reply. His answer ended the back-and-forth, carrying far greater weight than anyone else's in the room. "Edna Jenkins was tested while she was still alive, and the others were tested post-mortem in the autopsy."

"They tested the eighty-three year old grandma for AIDS?" David couldn't help but laugh a little bit as he envisioned Edna's doctors telling her family that the old lady might be HIV positive.

Isaac knew what David was grinning about, and in any other situation he might have also thought it was funny. But there was nothing funny about anything related to these patients and this deadly illness. "Apparently, one of her physicians had previously done work in sub-Saharan Africa and seen a lot of AIDS cases," Isaac explained. "My gut says that the fact that Mr. Gray had HIV is just a coincidence. Put in on the board anyway as a possibility, Leah," he said as a concession to both Anthony and David.

Isaac then turned his attention back to Dr. Pingrey. "Did Andrew die the same way as the others?"

****

"Do you think it's the HIV?"

Dr. Lucy Chang was standing just outside the closed door of her patient's hospital room and talking with a pathology specialist from UC-San Francisco. She had asked the other doctor to come and look at Andrew Gray's file. After examining her thirty-year-old patient yet again, this time with the infectious disease expert present, Dr. Chang was still no closer to figuring out what was killing Mr. Gray.

"I don't think so," the pathologist replied as he flipped through Patient Gray's chart one more time. "He wasn't aware that he was HIV positive, and he said that he was tested just last year. It typically takes around a decade for untreated HIV to progress into full-blown AIDS, and even then the person has at least another six months left." The doctor shook his head. "No, I don't think it's that. This guy was infected within the last year and was otherwise perfectly healthy, until two weeks ago when he managed to get himself beat up by Super Granny. A week later he's back in the hospital with severe joint pain, night sweats, a fever, and a rash. And now he's knocking on death's door? No," he concluded, flipping the chart closed and handing it back to Dr. Chang. "It's not the HIV. I don't know what it is, but it's not that."

NINETEEN

Having gone through the first batch of patient files with his new medical team, Isaac arrived at work early the next morning ready to dive in. He always felt this way at the beginning of a project: nervous, to be sure, but mostly excited. The thrill of the chase, the race against the clock, the challenge of knowing he was literally dealing in matters of life and death . . . that was what got Dr. Carlson's blood pumping. The excitement at the beginning of a case was only surpassed by the euphoria at the end when the mystery was finally solved. Isaac loved saving lives. So maybe it gave him a little bit of a God complex. Was that really such a bad thing? Not in Isaac's mind, it wasn't. Especially not when that complex also gave him the confidence to perform his medical miracles.

Isaac was surprised to discover that he was not the first member of the task force in the office that morning. Leah Mann was already there. Not wanting to startle the younger woman, Isaac cleared his throat loudly to announce his presence in the doorway of her lab.

Despite his efforts, the skittish Dr. Mann still jumped when she heard the noise. Leah quickly swung her head around and relief washed over her face when she saw who it was.

"Oh, Dr. Carlson, it's just you."

"How many times do I have to tell you to call me Isaac before you finally will?" he asked as he entered the room full of black tables, microscopes, and various other kinds of research machinery.

"Sorry," Leah replied, lowering her eyes. "I'll work on it . . . *Isaac.*"

"Good. Now what are you doing here so early?"

Leah responded with unexpected spunk: "one could ask you the same thing."

"I always get here at seven-thirty," Isaac answered smoothly.

"Oh." Again Leah lowered her eyes, as if to hide. "I just wanted to get a head start on the day. Sometimes I feel like I won't really be contributing anything to the task force since you all know so much more than me."

Isaac was surprised by Leah's admission. Not exactly sure how to handle delicate emotions when they didn't belong to a patient, he simply replied: "don't be ridiculous. I wouldn't have put you on the task force if I didn't think you could pull your weight."

Leah smiled nervously. "Yeah, I guess you're right."

Isaac turned to leave and go to his own research area when Leah stopped him. "Umm, Dr., I mean, Isaac. Do you have a minute?"

"What is it?"

The young woman was practically shaking because she was so nervous. "It's just that –"

"Yes?" prompted Isaac impatiently.

"It's just that I've never actually done this before," Leah confessed. "I usually work with creating new vaccines or researching a disease's global impact. I've never actually had to fight an active virus before. What am I supposed to do?"

Isaac took a long look at the novice doctor standing before him in her usual attire of baggy jeans, white sneakers, and an ill-fitting short-sleeve shirt. If not for the lab coat she was wearing, no one would have ever suspected her of being a board-certified immunologist. The woman shifted back and forth nervously while she awaited her group leader's response.

"Anthony never taught you how to make a test to screen for a bacterium or virus?" Isaac finally asked.

"Nuh-uh," she answered. "That's not really the kind of research that we do."

Isaac massaged the back of his neck with his head. "No, I suppose it wouldn't be." He took a deep breath, then said: "let me go drop off my briefcase in my office and then I'll come back and we can do a quick lesson before everybody else starts arriving."

Leah nodded her head and smiled in thanks. Not only would Isaac help her, but he would help her without anyone else around so no one would see that she hadn't known what to do. Maybe Keri was right. Maybe Isaac was a decent guy after all.

****

Dr. Carlson returned a few minutes later, bringing with him an old pathology textbook that he kept in his office.

"Take a seat," Isaac instructed, gesturing toward a stool by a work table. When Leah was seated, Isaac rolled another stool over to sit beside her.

"First of all," he said, placing the large textbook on the table in front of them, "read this when you go home tonight. It will help you be better informed and will probably also help you fall asleep."

The young doctor laughed. "Okay."

"Now," Isaac continued, "the first thing we'll need to do is figure out exactly what we're dealing with. The hospitals that treated our patients ran all kinds of tests, but to no avail. Nonetheless, we need to start over from scratch."

"Why?" Leah asked.

"Honestly? Because I don't trust that those other doctors did everything correctly," Isaac answered with a sigh. "We need to run every test, check every nook and every cranny to make sure that nothing was overlooked."

"Alright," responded Leah, nodding her head. "What's next after that?"

"We'll have to figure out if the illness we're dealing with is a bacterium or a virus. Which overall kind of illness it is will make a huge difference in our approach." Isaac already had a pretty good idea that it was a virus, but he didn't want to bias his co-workers' opinions. And they needed to double check the patients' blood samples anyway. "As you know," he went on, "bacterial cells are usually very easy to spot and much easier to treat than a virus. To be honest, if it is a bacteria and nobody figured that out yet then we have some pretty stupid doctors in this country."

Leah laughed because she thought she was expected to, but then quickly stifled the noise when she realized that Isaac was completely serious. Struggling to find the right words, she finally just said: "okay."

At this point, Dr. Carlson was talking more to himself than anyone else and didn't seem to notice Leah's uncomfortable moment. "Bacteria," he continued, "are noted for their unicellular, localized infections and their ability to be treated with antibiotics. Viruses, on the other hand, are usually systemic in the patient's body and cannot be counteracted by antibiotics."

"Right," Leah agreed. "We have vaccines to prevent the spread of a virus, and antiviral drugs can slow their progress, but once a virus takes hold we more or less have to let it run its course."

It was clear from the look on his face that Isaac didn't know what to think about Leah interrupting him. "I thought you said you didn't know what you were doing?"

"I don't," she quickly clarified. "I mean I know the difference between bacteria and viruses, but I don't know how to do any of the tests that you said we need to run."

Isaac sighed as he stood up from his stool. "Alright, why don't you just observe what I'm doing then? That'll probably be better than me trying to explain it to you."

****

A few days and a few dozen tests later, Isaac, Leah, and the rest of the NIH-CDC-Hopkins task force felt confident in their conclusion that the illness they were battling was a virus. Figuring that out, though, was the easy part. New viruses were being created every day in gene therapy labs around the world, so it wasn't like Isaac's team could just go down a list of known viruses until they found the one that matched their patients' symptoms. No, it was much more complicated than that.

Virus testing, as the doctors all knew, is accomplished through a process called PCR, or polymerase chain reaction. Developed in the mid- to late-1990s, PCR helps determine which viral genes are in the patient's blood. Another available technique, one that Isaac planned to use, was called the ELISA. A highly sensitive test, ELISA gained widespread popularity among doctors when it began to be used to screen for HIV. It is also common with workplace drug testing. In an ELISA test, the patient's serum is diluted and put on a plate along with antigens of whatever virus was being tested for. If that same virus' antibodies are present in the patient's body, then the antigens and antibodies would bind together. The process is repeated several times, with the result being a number . . . higher meaning positive, lower meaning negative.

Isaac and the five other doctors working in the NIH's third floor lab would be the first to admit that what they were doing wasn't particularly flashy or exciting. A lot of test tubes, a lot of culture trays, a lot of staring down into microscopes and watching centrifuges spin. The turnaround for each PCR or ELISA test was twenty-four to forty-eight hours, meaning that the work was also extremely time consuming. Time that the researchers knew they couldn't afford to waste, since each passing day seemed to bring news of yet another infected patient. Nevertheless, the presidentially-appointed task force soldiered on, fully confident that if they kept at it they would eventually find the answer they were all looking for.

TWENTY

"We need to recap," Isaac declared. The members of the task force were back in the white washed walls of the conference room – their first group meeting in seven days. "We've been in the lab for the past week . . . let's get caught up and get everything on the board so we know where we stand."

Without even being asked, Leah rose from the table and resumed her position at the giant whiteboard that covered an entire wall of the room, dry-erase marker in hand.

"Where should we start?" asked Isaac. "Patients or virus?"

"Patients," David answered as he shrugged off his suit jacket and rolled up his shirt sleeves to settle in for the long haul.

"Agreed," added Keri. "Let's get the emotional part over with so we can focus on medicine after that."

Isaac pursed his lips together and half rolled his eyes at his assistant. "How many times have I told you to not get so attached to the patients?"

"You're the one who makes us learn all of their names," Keri shot back.

Anthony nodded his head in agreement. "She has a point, Isaac."

"Whatever," the group leader sighed. "Let's just get started."

Leah knew that was her cue and began to read from the board next to her. "Patient number one: Edna Jenkins. Eighty-three years old from Colorado. Originally admitted after a car accident; readmitted a week later with a cough and a fever. Edna died eight days after that."

When none of the doctors seated at the conference table said anything, Dr. Mann continued down her list.

"Patient number two: Taylor Stone. Seventeen from Houston. In the hospital for chemotherapy treatments. Taylor's virus symptoms started with a sore throat and a headache, quickly progressing to nausea and extreme joint pain. Taylor died four days after her symptoms first appeared."

Isaac nodded his head while listening to the information. "Good. Well, not good, obviously. I meant continue," he clarified.

Leah took it all in stride. After working on the task force for a full week, she was used to Dr. Carlson's mind sometimes getting ahead of his speech. "Patient number three," she went on, "was also from Texas. Thomas George; forty-eight years old. He had an outpatient blood transfusion to help treat a MRSA infection. Cough, fever, and a rash appeared a week after the transfusion."

"So we're looking at a one week incubation period," commented Gill. "Damn, that's not a lot of time." The silence in the room simply confirmed Dr. Pingrey's opinion. "Sorry, Leah, keep going."

"Mr. George was admitted to the hospital ten days after his transfusion. He died forty-eight hours after that."

"Yep," Isaac acknowledged. "Next."

"Juan Sosa. Thirty-nine from Florida. Was undergoing treatment for stomach cancer. Standard one week incubation period and died two and a half weeks after his transfusion."

"Same symptoms?" asked Keri, taking notes in her binder.

"Same symptoms," Leah replied. "Fever, cough, fatigue, joint pain, skin lesions. Mr. Sosa's cause of death is listed as multiple organ failure." Dr. Mann flipped to the next page of her notebook, tastelessly labeled on the front as 'Victims' and then hastily crossed-through and replaced with 'Patients.'

"Wait," Anthony interrupted. "I thought the guy in San Francisco, Andrew Gray, was number four."

"That's what we thought originally," David agreed. "But Sosa's case was sent to us after we put out the CDC advisory, and he died before the San Francisco dude."

"Oh, okay," Anthony said, scribbling notes on his own legal pad. "Keep 'em coming, Leah."

"Next we do have Andrew Gray. Thirty years old and lived in San Francisco. Admitted to the hospital after being beaten up by an elderly woman who he tried to rob. . . . serves him right."

"We can do without the commentary, Dr. Mann," Isaac chastised.

"Sorry," she blushed. "Mr. Gray was readmitted to San Francisco General a week later, slipped into a fever-induced coma after another six days, and died five days after that. His cause of death was listed as organ failure."

"What about the HIV?" Dr. Russo chimed in. "He tested positive, right?"

"Right now I think we're treating that as a coincidence," Keri answered. She liked Anthony Russo – he was kind, well-mannered, and a legend in the field after his early work with the AIDS epidemic. Given his background, it was natural that the similarities between the two illnesses would stand out to him. Nevertheless, she replied – "his symptoms are the same as the others and he's the only one so far who has been HIV positive."

Just as Leah was about to begin describing the next patient on her list, a stopwatch started beeping loudly. "Sorry, that's mine," Gill said quickly. "I have a couple of tests running and had to set a timer for when they would be finished. I know this meeting is important –" he added, beginning to rise from his chair.

"No, no, you're right," Isaac told him. "Go check on that. This stuff can wait. In fact, let's all just get back to the lab. We'll do more of a recap later."

The group all began to stand and prepare to leave the conference room when suddenly Isaac stopped them.

"Wait. Leah, go back to the board," Isaac said, the urgency in his voice creating a palpable tension in the room.

"What is it, Isaac?" David asked.

"Hold on," Dr. Carlson responded, "I've got something." His task force deputies could almost literally see the wheels turning in his head as their boss tried to figure out whatever it was that had caught his attention.

"Our first patient, Edna Jenkins," Isaac began as he stood up and walked to the whiteboard himself. "What was her underlying problem?"

"Umm . . . she was in a car wreck," Leah answered after she found Edna's column on the board.

"She had surgery, right?" Isaac asked. "Does her file say anything about administering units of blood?"

David Malhotra hurriedly searched through the piles of medical folders strewn across the conference table until he found the one he was looking for. "Yes," he answered. "They gave her two units of blood because she lost so much in the car crash."

"And patient number two?" Isaac went on. "Taylor Stone? What about her . . . any blood given?"

David could tell that his NIH counterpart was on the verge of a big breakthrough. Locating Taylor's file, Dr. Malhotra quickly flipped to the appropriate page. "Yes. Multiple transfusions as part of her chemotherapy treatment."

"That's it!" Isaac exclaimed. He slammed his fist against the whiteboard in exuberant celebration. "That's it!" he repeated to his startled and confused task force team. "It's the blood. The virus is in the blood. All of our patients received blood transfusions for their underlying medical problem. It's in the blood."

TWENTY-ONE

"Dr. Carlson? Daniel Bader here. Richard Hughes' Chief of Staff."

It was only the second week of the task force's work, and Isaac was immediately puzzled as to why the President's top aide would be calling him. Isaac already knew that he was supposed to give a weekly update via email to the Deputy Chief of Staff, but he had never interacted with this Daniel Bader before and certainly hadn't expected a phone call from him.

"Yes, this is Dr. Carlson. What can I do for you?" Isaac asked.

A deep voice on the other end of the phone line replied: "I like that, Carlson. Cutting straight to the chase. We're going to get along just fine."

"Umm . . . I hope so," a still-confused Isaac responded.

"Listen," the Chief of Staff went on, "I've got our Communications Director here with me in my office, and we think it would be good if you set up a press conference over there at the National Institutes of Health. We're starting to get a lot of questions about patients dying from this mysterious illness, and we want you – as head of the task force we created to fight this thing – to get in front of a camera, say a few words, and reassure the public."

"Reassure them of what?" Isaac didn't mean for his question to come across as caustic as it did, but he was at the end of another very long day in the lab and really didn't have time for public relations gimmicks.

"Reassure them that you have the situation under control," Daniel Bader answered, his voice losing a touch of its earlier friendliness and now sounding more like the extremely powerful political giant that he was.

"Dr. Carlson? This is Dale Austin, White House Communications Director. Look, we're not talking about anything big. We can even say that you won't be taking any questions and you'll just read a statement. Like Daniel said, we just want you to reassure the public that everything is under control."

Isaac took a deep breath this time before speaking in order to make sure he kept his composure. Every so often he would have to attend meetings with politicians, mostly about NIH funding, and they never went well. *Politicians know absolutely nothing about medicine*, he thought for the ten thousandth time.

"The problem," Isaac finally replied slowly, "is that we don't have everything under control. I've got a stack of patient files that only keeps growing, a list of symptoms that make absolutely no sense, and a disease with a survival rate of zero percent. *Zero*," he said with emphasis. "Pardon my language, but right now my team and I don't have a fucking clue. We've only just now figured out that it's a blood-borne virus, but we don't know what the virus is, how to test for it, or how to treat it. Furthermore, we know it's in the bloodstream but we don't know how it's getting there. Is this a spontaneous mutation of some kind? Is there a patient zero somewhere spreading it? Is someone tampering with the nation's blood supply? We don't know. We just don't know."

When the two men he was talking to didn't immediately respond, Isaac continued: "now, gentlemen, if you want me to stand up in front of a bunch of reporters and tell them what I just told you, I'm happy to do it. But I won't lie and say we're winning this fight when we're not."

There was another pause on the other end of the line before the Chief of Staff finally said: "on further consideration, maybe a press conference isn't a great idea after all."

One perk of the conversation being over the phone instead of in person was that Isaac could roll his eyes, bob his head, and sarcastically mouth the words 'no shit' without the other two men knowing it.

"Oh, Isaac, one more thing," Daniel Bader added. "After you and your crew have been at it for a little while, maybe after you – how did you put it – get a fucking clue, the President wants you and someone from the CDC to come up to the White House to brief him on your progress. Someone will call later to set that up."

"Okay, sounds good," Isaac answered. *A face-to-face meeting with the President? Don't mind if I do.*

****

The morning after his conversation with Isaac Carlson, Daniel Bader was still thinking about what the doctor said on the phone. 'Is someone tampering with the nation's blood supply? We don't know.'

Tampering with the blood supply? Daniel didn't want to jump to any conclusions, didn't want to prematurely set off any alarms, because the minute this thing changed from just some random virus to a potentially intentional act, the entire game changed. Then it wasn't just a Health and Human Services project being run by a group of six doctors in a building in Bethesda. Then it became a terrorism investigation, which meant Department of Defense, Department of Homeland Security, and a level of public panic unlike anything anyone had ever seen. It meant hospitals were no longer safe. Blood supplies could no longer be trusted. In short, it meant a nightmare.

There would be no way to un-push that button, which was why Daniel wanted to be very cautious about pushing it in the first place.

"Allison!" he called out to his assistant. "Get me the FBI Director on the phone." Thinking about it for a second, he called out again. "Change that. Tell the Director I need to see him in my office. Immediately."

TWENTY-TWO

"Let me get this straight," Jack Leyton said, holding his hands out in the air. It was now 9:45 in the morning and FBI Director Leyton was seated in Daniel Bader's office, having just been informed by the White House Chief of Staff about his blood supply poisoning theory. "There's a virus out there," the Mr. Clean look-alike, West Point graduate summarized, "and it's killing people. Killing them fast. We've already got a team of doctors working on solving this thing, but now you want the Bureau to investigate if someone is deliberately poisoning America's blood supply?"

"Yes," Daniel answered without hesitation.

"I don't know, Bader," the Director replied, shaking his head. "We go back a long time, and you know I trust your judgment, but this just seems a little crazy to me. I mean, the logistics behind it, the medical expertise required to pull off something like that . . ."

"I know," the Chief of Staff said in agreement. "Trust me, I know. Humor me, though, will you? Pick out an agent who can be trusted with sensitive information and have him or her look into it. See if it would even be possible."

Jack Leyton nodded his head. "Okay. I'll have somebody look into it. Like my wife says, better safe than sorry."

Daniel laughed as he stood up and shook the Director's hand in thanks. "My wife says that all the time too." Again he laughed, then added with a sarcastic shake of his head: "women."

****

"Agent White!"

No further instructions were issued, but veteran FBI agent Reagan White knew what to do anyway. The gruff voice calling out to her was her boss, and he wanted her to come to his office. *Nevermind the fact that he has a phone, an email account, and an inner-office instant message system all at his disposal,* the strawberry blonde woman thought as she stood up behind her desk and straightened out her standard-issue, off-the-rack black pantsuit. *He'd rather yell across the entire building.* Reagan shook her head at her boss' antics as she made her way past cubicles full of busy workers to the corner office occupied by Bruce Molina, the Assistant Deputy Director of Major Crimes. Reagan always thought his title made her boss sound more important than he actually was, but of course she never said so.

"Yes sir?" Agent White asked, shoving her hands in her pockets and shifting her balance on to one leg more than the other. "What can I do for you?"

Without even looking up, the white-haired Clint Eastwood look-alike replied: "shut the door."

Reagan White's face crinkled up in confusion as she did what she was told. She hadn't heard of any big cases coming down the pipeline, and her boss only made her close the door if it was something important.

"Sit down, White," the Assistant Deputy Director ordered. A lifelong Democrat and, as he put it, a closeted hippie, Molina had refused to call Reagan by her first name ever since he learned that her parents – lifelong Republicans – had named their daughter after President Ronald Reagan.

It wasn't until after Agent White was seated that her boss finally looked up and made eye contact with her. "You've got a new assignment," he said, rummaging through piles of paperwork to find the correct file. After locating what he was looking for, Molina handed the black file folder across the table to his best field agent. "All of the information you need to get started is in there."

"What about my other cases?" Reagan asked.

"Reassign what you can, but the rest will have to wait. This one," he said, nodding his head toward the file in her hand, "came down straight from the top."

Reagan nodded her ponytailed head in acknowledgment of her instructions. She started to get up to leave but was stopped by her boss.

"Oh, one more thing, White. That big red 'CONFIDENTIAL' stamp on the folder isn't just for show. Nobody knows about this. Nobody even knows you're working on something you can't talk about. Got it?"

"Yes sir," the ten-year Bureau veteran answered. "Got it."

"Good. Now get out of here and go to work."

****

It was a delicate feat of strength and balance that enabled Reagan White to climb the four flights of narrow stairs leading to her apartment without dropping the two bankers boxes she was carrying, one under each arm. The fact that it had rained that day and the prewar building's floors were made of marble didn't help either.

After what seemed like the equivalent of climbing Mt. Everest, Reagan finally reached the fourth floor landing and immediately dropped both of the paperwork-laden boxes on the floor. At this point, after yet another fourteen-hour day, if something in the boxes had broken in their fall . . . so be it.

The tall and lanky FBI agent struggled to catch her breath as she rummaged through the briefcase on her shoulder to find her apartment keys. No matter how many times she climbed those stairs (seemingly millions), the four flights still kicked her butt. Finally finding her keys,

Reagan unlocked the door, swung it open, and then used a combination of kicking and shoving to get the two heavy boxes inside her apartment.

Even though Mr. Molina, her boss, had only given her one small folder worth of material, the boxes that Reagan had driven out to Bethesda to retrieve contained the information she really needed to know about her new assignment: patient files. Or, rather, copies of patient files to be exact. Nine hospital patients had come down with some mystery virus, and now Reagan's superiors wanted her to investigate – quietly – whether the people were being infected on purpose.

How the heck am I supposed to know? she thought yet again as she left the boxes just inside the door and made her way down the short hallway to her living room.

"Hey Ari," Reagan said cheerfully to the large Persian cat sprawled across the back of the couch. Ari, short for Aristotle, barely raised his oversized head in acknowledgement of his owner's arrival. Reagan often thought that Ari would be the perfect example for anyone wanting to prove that cats have attitude problems. But she loved him dearly anyway. He was named after the philosopher, but for an unusual reason. Reagan adopted Ari from the local shelter the previous year on March 22nd – 3/22 – and the human Aristotle died in 322 BC. A professor of Reagan's in college always asked students when certain philosophers died, most commonly Aristotle, which was why she still remembered the date. It was a way for Reagan to honor her professor in a way, even though he was outgoing and very kind while Aristotle the cat was, well, a tyrant.

"But you're *my* little tyrant. Isn't that right, Ari?" Reagan called out from her bedroom as she changed out of her horribly uncomfortable suit and into oversized sweatpants and a FBI t-shirt. Walking back to the living room, Agent White patted her grumpy-yet-lovable cat on the head as she entered into a staring contest with the bankers boxes by her front door.

Less-than-thrilled was definitely an accurate description for her feelings about this new assignment. It seemed like a wild goose chase to her. And Reagan had been around the Bureau long enough to recognize a wild goose when she saw one. Indeed, White should have been the one sending others on goose chases by now. But Reagan loved her work. Solving crimes, being out in the field, interacting with victims and witnesses – that was what got her up in the mornings . . . not sitting behind a desk in a stuffy office all day. So she turned down offers for promotion and their accompanying pay raises, and stuck with her Agent title and fourth-floor walk-up. "But we'll never have to buy a Stairmaster living here, will we?" Reagan asked Aristotle, who meowed in response and rolled over to nap on his other side.

Reagan took a deep breath and exhaled loudly. "Might as well get started. The sooner I catch the goose the sooner I can go back to working on real cases." Like the stabbing by the National Mall, or the shooting near the Potomac River's waterfront. Real cases; not running errands because some member of the FBI brass had seen *Contagion* one too many times and got spooked by this new virus.

TWENTY-THREE

The first thing on Reagan's to-do list for the next day was to put in a call with Dr. Isaac Carlson, the head of the task force trying to find a cure for the virus. She wanted to meet with him in person and try to get a better sense of what exactly she was working with. Or, more accurately, what she was working against.

Having checked that first item off her list, Reagan then turned her sights to the CDC. Her boss had told her that the theory was that someone was poisoning America's blood supply, and Reagan needed to learn more about where that supply was and who controlled it.

As expected, no one at the CDC was available to talk to her, but Reagan left a message anyway. They worked for the government, after all. Same team. Surely someone would help her out.

****

A little over two hours later, Reagan's office phone rang. "Reagan White, FBI."

"Hi, Agent White. This is Dr. Eileen Billings at the CDC. I work in the Infectious Disease Pathology Branch of the Division of High-Consequence Pathogens and Pathology. I understand you called earlier looking for help with one of your investigations?"

"Oh, yes, hi," Reagan replied excitedly. "Thank you so much for calling me back."

"Not a problem," said the friendly voice on the other end of the line. "How can I help?"

"Well, Dr. –" Reagan paused, momentarily forgetting the woman's name.

"Billings," the doctor filled in. "Eileen Billings."

"Right. I'm so sorry. Dr. Billings. I've been assigned to investigate a virus that is affecting people around the country, and I'm hoping you can provide me with a little bit of background information about our blood supply and how one might gain access to it."

"Sure, I'm happy to help," Dr. Billings responded. "I'm curious, though. Why didn't you just call my boss? I'm pretty sure you two are working on the same thing."

"Your boss?" asked Reagan, confused.

"Yeah, David Malhotra. He's head of my division here at the CDC and was sent up to the NIH near Washington to be on a virus task force."

"The task force being led by Dr. Isaac Carlson?"

"That's the one."

Reagan issued a slight laugh. "Oh, I'm sorry. I didn't know that. I'm hoping to meet with Dr. Carlson soon. But maybe since I already have you on the phone I could go ahead and ask you a few questions?"

"Fine with me," the other woman replied. Reagan could almost hear her friendly smile through the receiver.

"Awesome. I really appreciate it. Umm," the agent began inarticulately, "this may sound like a dumb question, but where do we keep our blood? Is there like a Fort Knox for blood?"

Dr. Billings laughed. "No, no, nothing like that. Some donated blood is kept at hospitals, and a lot I believe is at big warehouse-type facilities run by the Red Cross. In fact," the woman added, "not that I'm not willing to answer your questions, but you'd probably get better answers if you just contacted the Red Cross directly. They handle the vast majority of blood donations in the United States."

"Okay, yeah. I'll do that. Thanks, Dr. Billings."

"Well I didn't do much, but you're welcome anyway."

It was now Reagan's turn to smile. "You pointed me in the right direction. Definitely worthy of a thanks."

"Happy to help. And good luck with everything, Agent White. That virus is a mean SOB."

"Thanks," Reagan responded. "I'll keep that in mind." The two women then ended their conversation, and no sooner had she hung up with the CDC then did Reagan pick up the phone once again to call the Red Cross.

****

He looks about as happy to be having this meeting as I do, Reagan thought as the gray haired, spectacled doctor walked down a hallway toward where she was waiting in the entrance lobby of the National Institutes for Health. This was Reagan's second visit to the Bethesda campus in three days: the day before yesterday to pick up the heavy boxes containing copies of the patient files, and today to interview the man in charge of the medical side of the investigation. This Dr. Carlson character – he of the brooding stare, lab coat, dress shirt, and slacks – was supposedly the best in his business. Which was good, because Reagan knew next to nothing about medicine and definitely needed to have some of the more technical things explained to her. *For starters*, she thought, *how would an attack like the one I'm investigating even be possible?*

****

Isaac glanced over his shoulder at the slender FBI agent following him from the lobby to the elevator bank so they could go meet in his office. The strawberry blonde woman had introduced herself as Reagan White and was as tall as he was while wearing flat shoes. *Ugly flat shoes*, he thought with a look of disdain. Isaac was no fashion aficionado, that was for sure, but he knew enough to at least look somewhat in style. *She clearly goes for comfort over fashion.*

The elevator ride up to the third floor and the short walk to Isaac's office passed without any comment between the two, with both wondering why the other didn't seem to want to be having this meeting. The always-curious pathologist opened with that exact question.

"So, Agent White," Isaac began, taking a seat behind his desk and motioning for her to do the same in a chair opposite him, "I know why I don't want to be meeting with you. What is your reason for not wanting to meet with me?"

His question clearly took the agent by surprise. "Umm, well," Reagan answered slowly, "to be honest, I think I've been sent on a bit of a wild goose chase. But," she declared as she pointed her finger at Isaac, "I didn't say that."

"Say what?" he asked, and it again took Agent White a second to catch up to the speed at which Isaac's brain functioned. When Reagan finally realized the meaning behind the question, she smiled.

"Exactly. I didn't say anything."

Reagan then shifted in her seat and crossed one long leg over the other before saying: "what about you, Dr. Carlson? Why don't you want to be talking to me right now?"

"Call me Isaac, please," he replied, turning on the same charm that always made him a favorite with patients. "And I don't know if you're on a wild goose chase or not." Isaac paused to rub his hand back and forth through his hair. "But I do know that my time would be better spent in my lab trying to fight this virus rather than sitting here reviewing patient files with you."

Isaac didn't mean for his comment to sound condescending, and he breathed a sigh of relief when the woman's freckled face showed no signs of his words having come across that way.

"Well, in that case," Reagan replied, "I'll try to keep this as short as possible." She then took a legal pad and pen out of her briefcase and set them on her lap. "What I need most from you, Dr. – *Isaac*, is an explanation of how a deliberate poisoning like this would even be medically possible."

Isaac interrupted her. "Is that what the feds are saying? It's a deliberate poisoning?"

Reagan looked back at him confusedly. "You're saying it isn't?"

"I'm saying I don't know. It's one of the possibilities that we've considered, but it's not like it's the front-runner."

"Well, someone somewhere thinks it's the front-runner," Reagan responded with a sigh. "But it seems rather far-fetched to me. I mean, for starters, I've read through the patient files and none of them seem to have anything in common, but shouldn't they be related somehow? Isn't that how these things work?"

Isaac thought about his answer for a minute. "For new diseases, or what looks like new mutations on a preexisting disease, there's usually a patient zero. For example, a man named Gaëtan Dugas was popularly labeled 'patient zero' for AIDS because of his connection to so many of the early cases in the United States."

"So I should be looking for a patient zero here? I've been trying to find any connections or patterns between patients, but like I said I've got nothing so far."

"We *might* be looking for a patient zero," Isaac clarified. "I don't know for sure. And even if that is what, or rather who, we're looking for, patients zero can often be off-the-radar. Maybe we're looking for someone who we haven't identified as being infected by the virus."

"Okay . . ." Reagan replied. "Aside from that, maybe you could go into a little bit of detail about the medical side of things?"

"You want me to translate the case files into English for you, right?"

Reagan smiled again. She liked this guy's style. "Yes please."

Isaac let loose a short laugh as he leaned back in his chair and put his hands behind his head. "Well, to begin with, there are three big questions to ask when talking about whether or not deliberately poisoning the blood supply with a virus is far-fetched. The first," he said, "is if it's possible to create a new virus from scratch. And the answer to that is yes." Isaac leaned forward again and placed his forearms on his desk. "Researchers in labs make new viruses – what we call recombinant viruses – all the time. It's done a lot for gene therapy and things like that."

"Oh, okay," Reagan replied. "What's the second question?"

"What would it take to create the kind of virus we're dealing with, which is A) untraceable," Isaac said as he counted off the characteristics with his fingers, "and B) untreatable."

"What do you mean by untraceable?"

"Well, that gets us into the third question about logistics. Even after the virus is made, the person or people who created it will still have to find a way to get the infected blood into the hospitals' blood banks without getting caught."

Reagan huffed out a breath in response. "So I was right. It is far-fetched."

Isaac nodded. "Far-fetched? Yes. Impossible? No."

"Alright," Reagan said with a renewed determination, "let's just go with this for a minute. We've got somebody, or a group of somebodies, wanting to make a new virus. What did you mean when you said it's untreatable?"

"Stop me at any point if I switch from English over into doctor-speak, okay?" With a nod of Reagan's head in agreement, Isaac began his explanation.

"Viruses are created by taking a vector, which is like a capsule or a shell, and filling that vector with DNA or RNA that will turn into proteins. So the one my task force and I are dealing with has deadly proteins."

"Okay, I'm with you so far," Reagan said.

"When a patient comes in with a viral illness, we try to figure out what the virus is by looking at what cells are affected."

"How do you know that?" asked the FBI agent.

"Their symptoms," answered the doctor. "Then we take tissue samples from those affected cells and look at them under a microscope to try to see any virus particles. Also important is a genetic technique called PCR, followed by sequencing."

"Do I need to know what 'PCR' stands for?"

"No," Isaac replied with a grin. "Just know that during those tests we're comparing the genetic sequence of this virus with the known sequences of other viruses to see what family it belongs to."

"Virus families," Reagan repeated, shaking her head. "Not something I ever thought I'd be talking about." She paused. "Sorry. Keep going."

"You really need to know all of this stuff?" Isaac asked skeptically.

"If my hypothetical bad guy needs to know it, then I need to know it," Agent White answered firmly.

"Okay. Well, to answer your question, this virus –"

"I heard someone on the news call it SuperAIDS," Reagan interrupted.

"Yeah . . . I've heard that too. I don't really like the term, because it's not AIDS. It's in the same family and also affects the patient's CD4 cell levels, but it's not AIDS."

Reagan quickly apologized.

"No, don't worry about it. Not a big deal," Isaac said dismissively. "Like I was saying, this virus is untraceable because it doesn't show up on any of the tests that the Red Cross and hospitals run on blood to make sure it's clean before it is used in a transfusion. So they have no way of knowing if the blood is tainted or not." Isaac paused before adding: "that's what I'm working on right now. A way to test blood for this virus."

"And the untreatable?" Reagan asked, remembering that they both wanted to keep this meeting short.

"That's pretty straightforward. We don't have a treatment. Everyone who has gotten the virus has died. We don't even have a way to slow down its progression."

Agent White noted the frustration in Dr. Carlson's voice as he talked about not being able to stop the virus from killing people. "So your only option," she asked, "is prevention with the test you're working on?"

"That's right," Isaac responded, nodding his head. "Any more questions?"

Reagan took that as Isaac's clear signal that he wanted the conversation to end. "Nope. Not right now." She smiled as she stood up from her chair and extended her arm to shake hands with the obviously brilliant man in front of her. "Thank you so much for your time. Keep me updated on your progress, yeah?"

"Will do," said Isaac. As he walked Agent White over to his office door and opened it, the doctor added: "you do the same. If it does turn out that there's some mad scientist running around killing people, I want to know about him."

TWENTY-FOUR

A few days after his meeting with the FBI agent, and no further along in his quest for a screening test for the virus, Isaac's cell phone buzzed loudly as it vibrated on his office desk. He normally turned the phone completely off when he was in research mode, since the slightest ding or buzz might cause him to lose a very important train of thought. And he needed those thoughts, especially right now as he worked to isolate exactly what was causing his patients to die. However, it was that same project which led Dr. Carlson to leave his phone on vibrate tonight, since any updates on new patients with the same mysterious illness would be sent directly to him.

The Blackberry buzzed again, then once more, getting perilously close to scooting itself right off the desk and onto the hard tile floor. Seeing that, Isaac quickly got up from his workstation and crossed his office to pick up the phone. As he suspected, the subject line of the incoming email was 'NEW PATIENT.' After clicking to open the document, Dr. Carlson quickly scanned for the information he was looking for.

To: Dr. Isaac Carlson, NIH
From: Dr. Craig Brooks
Re: NEW PATIENT

Dr. Carlson,
My name is Dr. Craig Brooks. I'm the Chief of Staff at Temple University Hospital in Philadelphia. We have a patient here who fits the symptom profile that the CDC sent out. Her name is Alicia Kendrick, she's thirty-three, and she initially came to us eight days ago with severe burns from a grease fire. Until yesterday Ms. Kendrick was undergoing treatment in our burn center, but we have since

moved her into an isolation room. Her symptoms include severe joint pain, persistent cough, blurred vision, and diarrhea.

Since you're the head of the task force for this illness, I'll leave it up to you what we should do next.

Best regards,
Craig Brooks, MD

Isaac didn't even hesitate before hitting reply:

Dr. Brooks, I'm coming to Philadelphia. For the love of God, just keep her alive until I get there.

****

The loud pounding sound on her front door startled Keri Dupree. It was ten thirty at night; no one in their right mind would be making such a racket, especially not in her quiet suburban neighborhood. She hit the 'mute' button on the television remote and listened as the banging continued.

"Stay here," Keri's husband commanded as he got out of bed and slipped on his robe and house shoes. Keri recognized that tone of voice – it meant that Scott meant business. He obviously didn't like this situation – it made him uneasy – and he wanted his wife upstairs and safe if anything did happen.

Keri heard Scott's feet on the stairs, but when the front door squeaked as it opened she breathed a sigh of relief. Her husband wouldn't open the door for someone he didn't know, especially not at this hour.

"Keri!" her husband yelled. She knew that voice too. Scott wasn't worried anymore. Now he was mad.

The accomplished doctor hurried to get dressed in her own robe and slippers and then headed down the hallway to the front stairs. When she reached the landing, Keri saw what had made her husband so angry. Or, rather, *who* had made him angry.

"Isaac, what on earth are you doing here?" Keri asked, folding her arms across her chest and refusing to go down the stairs. The way she figured, Isaac was here to tell her something, and then he would either leave or she would be changing clothes so she could go somewhere with him. Either way, Keri's next stop would be her bedroom so there was no reason to go downstairs. "You're going to wake up the whole neighborhood pounding on the door like that," she scolded her boss.

"Sorry," Isaac replied without an ounce of remorse in his voice. "But I need you. Now."

"Hold on just a second," Scott broke in, his frustration evident in his voice. "You can't just come barging into our house at all hours of the night demanding to see my wife. She's not your slave, Carlson."

Keri cringed at both the tone of her husband's voice and the anger that flashed across her boss' eyes.

"Your wife is a critical and integral member of a task force that is working to solve a national medical emergency. If you don't like the idea of her helping me, think of it as her helping America." Isaac smirked as he played the patriotism card. It worked every time. "Now c'mon, Keri. Go put on some real clothes. We need to hurry. We don't have much time."

On the outside, Dr. Dupree made an annoyed face, rolled her eyes, and sighed to express her irritation with her boss. But, on the inside, Keri was grinning from ear to ear and doing backflips. Isaac Carlson, Mr. Perfectionist I-Don't-Ever-Give-Compliments just told her husband that she was a "critical and integral" member of his task force. That America needed her help. It was sad, of course, how all of those people were mysteriously dying. But it was also the most exciting thing that Keri had worked on in years –

heck, it was the most exciting thing she'd ever worked on – and the fact that Isaac needed her help so urgently that he had risked a showdown with Scott to come get her made her insides beam with pride.

****

Scott Dupree blocked the bedroom doorway as his wife, now dressed in jeans, boat shoes, and a red fleece pullover with NIH monogrammed on the chest, went to leave. "You aren't seriously going with him right now, are you?" It was phrased as a question, but after six years of marriage Keri knew enough to recognize that it was more of an order. An order she had every intention of disobeying.

"Move, Scott. I need to go."

He didn't budge.

"I said *move*," Keri repeated as she lowered her shoulder and pushed past her husband. Without stopping or even turning her head, Keri called out to the glowering man standing behind her in their bedroom doorway: "I've never said a word when you sleep at the office during big trials. Not one word."

And with that, Keri followed Isaac out onto the porch and slammed the front door behind her.

TWENTY-FIVE

"This better be important, Isaac. You just caused a fight between Scott and me." The two doctors were now in Isaac's car headed north on Interstate-95.

"Very important," her boss responded as he rubbed one hand back and forth through his close-cropped hair in an attempt to wake himself up more. He was chock-full of adrenaline at the prospect of examining a patient who was still alive, but a two and a half hour drive in the middle of the night is rough on anybody. "We've got another patient. She's in Philadelphia."

"Wait, 'is' in Philadelphia?" Keri asked.

"Yep," Isaac grinned. "She's still alive."

****

Dr. Brooks, Temple University Hospital's Chief of Staff and the person who had emailed Isaac about the new patient, was waiting just inside his hospital's main entrance when Drs. Carlson and Dupree arrived just after 1:00am. With only the briefest of introductions, Dr. Brooks immediately started walking his guests in the direction of Alicia Kendrick's room. All three of them knew that there could be little time to spare.

"Has there been any change in her condition since you emailed me earlier?" Isaac asked.

"Not that we've noticed," replied Dr. Brooks. "Her temperature remains elevated but manageable. Our biggest task so far has been keeping her hydrated because of the diarrhea. We can't use any of the normal entry points for IV fluids because of the burns."

Dr. Brooks briefly stopped talking so he could punch a security code into a keypad on the wall. The letters on the double doors in front of them read 'RESTRICTED ACCESS' with two big red stop signs on either end of the writing.

The locks on the doors clicked open and Dr. Brooks pushed his way through, holding the door behind him for Isaac and Keri. "This is our isolation hall. Each room is sterile, sealed, and has its own ventilation system. And this," the chief added as he gestured to the room beside him, "is the patient I emailed you about. Alicia Kendrick."

"Can I see her chart?" asked Keri, determined to do more than simply be along for the ride.

"Sure," Dr. Brooks said, pulling a large patient file out of a cubby on the door and handing it to Dr. Dupree.

While Keri read through the pages, hoping to find something that the hospital staff overlooked, Isaac walked up to the glass window and looked in on the only known living victim of his enemy. It was a race against the clock, Isaac knew that; starting from scratch, trying to figure out what was making these people sick, and then creating a way to treat them.

This illness is my enemy, Isaac thought again, steeling himself for his first face-to-face encounter with a casualty of his war. *When I graduated from med school, Grandpa Carlson told me there would come a day when I'd finally meet my match with a case.* "I fought against enemies foreign in the Second World War," the old man had said. "And then I came home and fought enemies domestic as a police officer. But you, my boy, will face a different kind of enemy. It's foreign because it doesn't belong, but it's domestic because it's within us. But what's important, Isaac, is that you face it. You fight it. You don't run from it. You stick with it, and, eventually, you'll beat it.' *Oh Grandpa*, Isaac thought with a sigh. *I sure hope you were right about that last part. I don't know if I can beat this one.*

****

Keri and Isaac continued to pepper Dr. Brooks with questions about Alicia Kendrick as they scrubbed in and donned masks before entering the patient's sterilized room. Ms. Kendrick's regular attending physician had also joined the group, having been called in to the hospital despite the hour.

"What about lesions on her skin?" Keri asked. "That has been a common symptom with other patients."

"The problem with that," responded the head of the burn unit, "is that we have no idea what her actual skin looks like. The burns that put her in here in the first place would mask any lesions."

Isaac wasn't satisfied with that answer. "You're telling me you've checked every spot on her body? She wasn't burned on one hundred percent of her skin . . . she wouldn't be alive if she was. So what about the thirty percent that wasn't burned? Have you checked that?" Irritation rose in Isaac's voice as he continued grilling the other doctor. "Have you taken the time, when changing her bandages, to look for anything out of the ordinary on the burned skin? Well, have you?"

The burn unit doctor shoved his hands in his pockets and stubbed his toes into the floor, visibly embarrassed after being chastised by the visiting physician. "No sir," he said quietly.

"Well there's no time like the present to change that," declared Keri. She then stepped past the three men standing around her and pushed through the door to the patient's room.

TWENTY-SIX

Oh my God, Keri thought as she got her first up-close glimpse of the patient, Alicia Kendrick. *She looks like a mummy.*

Which was the truth. The grease fire that had quickly spread from her stove to the entire kitchen and enveloped Alicia in the process had left third-degree burns on approximately seventy percent of the woman's body. It looked like more than that right now, though, since Ms. Kendrick was laying face-up in the hospital bed and her back was significantly less burned than her front.

The mummy aspect of the situation wasn't what first caught Isaac's attention as he followed his deputy into the room. It was the smell. Isaac had done a burn unit rotation during his residency, and charred human flesh wasn't a smell that was easy to forget. Ever. Charcoal and sulfur and some particularly nauseating X factor; it was truly unlike anything else he had smelled before or after. So strong that it almost converted from a smell in his nose to a taste in his mouth.

Trying to distract his nose and the accompanying gag reflex, Isaac turned to Dr. Brooks. "Is she awake?"

A low groaning sound coming from the hospital bed answered Dr. Carlson's question for him. After the patient emitted another soft moan, the attending physician walked over to a chair in the corner and picked up a small black keyboard, returning to place it ever so gently on Alicia's lap.

Turning to the other doctors in the room, he explained: "the patient –"

"Ms. Kendrick," Isaac corrected.

"What?"

Keri jumped in to rescue the unsuspecting doctor from her boss' impending lecture about bedside manner and caring enough to learn people's names. "The patient has a name," Keri explained.

"Right. Of course she does," the attending answered, not quite understanding what had just happened. "Umm, so anyway, like I was saying, *Ms. Kendrick*, Alicia, is currently unable to speak because of her burns, but she has retained enough of her fine motor skills to be able to do a form of modified typing." Gesturing to the little black box resting on top of the patient's hospital-issue bed sheet, he added: "this keyboard is how we communicate. Alicia" – he used her name this time, catching on quickly – "types what she wants to say and it shows up on the big TV screen behind you."

Isaac and Keri turned around and looked up to see a fairly large flat screen television hanging from the wall. On the screen was a typed message: WHO ARE THESE PEOPLE?

Isaac took it upon himself to answer Alicia's question. "I'm Dr. Isaac Carlson, and this is my associate Dr. Keri Dupree. We're from the National Institutes of Health in Bethesda, Maryland."

"They're here to talk to you about the new symptoms you've been having," her regular doctor added. Keri was quick to notice how little the woman seemed to trust any of the new people in the room and how much faith was displayed in the looks that Alicia gave to the burn unit attending, a decent enough looking thirty-something who was sporting some combination of hipster and nerd-chic and had in all seriousness introduced himself as Dr. Rob.

Taking advantage of the silence after Dr. Rob's answer, Keri stepped forward. "I know it will be painful, but is it alright if I do a very quick examination? There are just a few things I want to check you for."

It took a minute for Keri to remember to turn around and check the TV for Alicia's reply. It read: WHAT KINDS OF THINGS?

"Skin lesions, mostly," Keri answered.

The next typed message revealed the patient's dark sense of humor as she put MY WHOLE BODY IS ONE BIG SKIN LESION.

Dr. Rob smiled gently at the woman who was only a few years younger than Keri and placed his hand just above her head on her pillow. "It'll just take a minute, Alicia."

Keri scoffed internally at the other doctor's words and the lack of any response from the hospital's chief. *No way in hell would Isaac ever let me act flirty like that with a patient. Courteous, yes. Nice, yes. But this guy looks like he's angling to score a date when she gets released from here.* A sadness clouded Keri's features as she realized that the patient in front of her would probably never leave this room, let alone this hospital, ever again. *If she's got the virus*, Keri thought, *she's already a goner.*

Turning to see where Alicia had put OKAY on the screen, Keri then walked to one side of the hospital bed as Isaac took his place on the other side.

"Just relax, Ms. Kendrick," Isaac said to the woman whose brunette beachy waves used to make other girls jealous but that the fire had reduced to a few small strands of charred hair on the back of her scalp. "Like Dr. Dupree said, we'll be very quick."

The fire victim slowly closed her eyes in anticipation of the pain that would surely come when the two doctors started poking and prodding what remained of her sensitive skin.

As Isaac gently pulled back some of the gauze covering Alicia's forearm, Keri trained her focus on the patient's face. There was one place she knew for sure wasn't burned, and that was the first spot she wanted to check.

"I'm just going to look at your gums for a minute," Keri announced before slowly prying open Alicia's mouth. What she saw confirmed the suspicions that Dr. Brooks had first raised in his email to Isaac. Small white pustules and lesions dotted the inner lining of her mouth – one of the common symptoms of AIDS and something that had been showing up with many of the task force's patients as well.

"Isaac," Keri said softly, nodding her head in the direction she wanted him to look. Pausing his examination of Alicia's forearm, Isaac stepped closer to her head and leaned forward to get a better look at what Keri was showing him. The pathologist then turned away so the patient couldn't see him, grimacing and giving a quick, confirming nod of his head to Dr. Books.

The hospital chief of staff's disappointment was evident on his face as he came to terms with the reality before him. Alicia Kendrick had the virus. She was going to die. And there was nothing that he or anyone else could do about it.

TWENTY-SEVEN

This is the worst part of the job, Reagan White thought as she slowly walked up the sidewalk toward the split-level house in front of her. It was never easy talking to victims' families. *Especially when you're the one who has to bring them more bad news.* In this instance, Agent White had to inform the family of the recently-deceased Mike Russell that he might have died as the result of an elaborate domestic terrorism plot.

Reagan took a deep breath and shook her shoulders to loosen them up before she rang the doorbell. She didn't really expect anyone to answer the door of the Russell's Baltimore home, but since this patient was so close to her office she figured it was worth the drive just in case.

Lost in her own thoughts, Reagan was surprised when a disheveled, brown-haired, middle-aged woman opened the door in an oversized bathrobe. "Can I help you?"

"Are you Mrs. Rebecca Russell?" Reagan asked.

The woman nodded in the affirmative. "I am."

Reagan knew her next few lines by heart; had said them way too many times while investigating way too many killings. "I'm so sorry to bother you, ma'am, but my name is Agent Reagan White. I'm with the –"

Just as she was about to say FBI, something strange happened. Reagan paused. She didn't want to tell Mrs. Russell the truth. Didn't want to add even more confusion and pain to an already grieving widow's life. So Reagan lied.

"I'm with the government. I was wondering if you have a few minutes to talk about your husband."

The other woman looked at her skeptically. *Can she tell I'm lying?* Reagan wondered. Then, nodding her head and stepping back from the door, Rebecca Russell invited her visitor to come inside.

"You said you're with the government?" Mrs. Russell asked as she sat down in an oversized recliner in her wallpapered living room.

"Yes ma'am," Reagan answered.

"What part?"

Reagan paused. She hated lying. "I'm working in conjunction with Health and Human Services on a case." *That's kind of true*, she thought. *HHS is looking into the virus, too.*

The widow seemed to accept Reagan's answer. "What does that have to do with my husband?"

It startled the FBI agent how easily the lies came now. "Doctors listed Mr. Russell's cause of death as unknown. Given the, umm, unique nature of his symptoms, HHS wanted to investigate a little further to make sure your husband wasn't caught up in some kind of outbreak."

Again, it was a half-truth, but it worked as Mrs. Russell nodded her head in understanding. "Yeah I heard something on the news about some mysterious new illness. Do you think my Mike had that?"

Reagan felt a sudden and unexpected pang of loneliness in her chest when the woman across the room from her said 'my Mike.' Agent White had never had anyone refer to her as 'my Reagan.' No one aside from her parents, anyway. She worked too much to ever meet anyone outside of the office, and at the Bureau she was always considered to be just one of the guys. Usually Reagan liked the equal treatment, but every once in a while – like now – Reagan felt overwhelmingly lonely.

Quickly snapping herself out of her pity party and back to the task at hand, the young woman answered: "it's possible he had that illness, yes ma'am."

It *was* possible. In fact, given all of the patient files that Reagan had read through, it was nearly a certainty that this woman's husband died of the mysterious virus. Trying to stay on track, Reagan continued:

"I don't want to take up too much of your time –"

"All I've got now is time, honey," Mrs. Russell interrupted.

Reagan nodded her head sympathetically. "Right. I'm sorry. I just have a few questions to ask you if that's alright."

"Sure. Go ahead."

The agent took a small notepad and pen out of her briefcase to record the widow's answers.

"Did your husband travel anywhere recently?"

"No. He needed a heart transplant. Of course he didn't travel anywhere."

"Oh, true. Of course. Umm . . . did your husband or do you personally know of anyone else who has died recently under the same circumstances?"

Mrs. Russell shook her head back and forth. "No."

"Have you or anyone else who had close contact with your husband travelled anywhere recently?"

Again the woman shook her head no.

"Okay," Reagan said, making a note on her paper. "One last question. Did you ever notice anyone suspicious hanging around the hospital?"

Rebecca Russell looked confused. "No . . . why would you ask that? It thought this was a virus?"

"It was. It is," Reagan said quickly. "That's just a standard thing I ask with every investigation." She knew that the question would raise the other woman's suspicion, but Reagan had to ask it anyway. Computer searches hadn't turned up any links between the patients, so if this was a planned attack then the only possibility that Reagan saw was someone going to the hospitals and poisoning the blood there.

Agent White could see Mrs. Russell eyeing her skeptically. *Time to wrap this up before I really blow my cover*, Reagan thought as she stood up off the couch where she had been sitting.

"Thank you so much for your time, ma'am. There's no need to get up; I can see myself out. And again," Reagan added, "I'm very sorry for your loss." Reagan then quickly walked out, her mind already on the next place she would visit as part of her investigation.

TWENTY-EIGHT

It didn't matter how tall she was (five feet, nine inches), how long she had been an FBI agent (ten years), or how many guns she was carrying (two – one on her hip and another at her ankle) – there were still certain situations that scared Reagan White. Like this one.

The manager of the New York City Red Cross blood bank in Queens had told her on the phone he would meet her after they closed for the night at six o'clock. Which was, unfortunately, after sunset. The distribution center wasn't exactly in the best part of town, either, which only added to Reagan's lingering paranoia about being out by herself after dark. "Better paranoid than dead" was what Mrs. White had always told her daughter, and Reagan still lived by that mantra.

Her left hand was resting on top of her holstered 9mm Glock as she opened the grungy, heavy door to the old warehouse-type building and walked inside an even grungier, dimly-lit lobby. With her eyes peeled and her head on a swivel, Reagan quickly crossed the empty foyer and was thankful that there was an elevator already waiting when she pushed the 'up' button.

****

"Agent White, I presume?" a white-haired man in khakis and a Red Cross embroidered golf shirt asked.

"That's me," Reagan nodded as she stepped farther away from the elevator and toward the two men standing by what looked like a receptionist's desk. *So this is the actual Red Cross office*, she thought while looking around at freshly-painted white walls and pictures of smiling doctors and patients. *You'd think they could get their landlord to do something about the rest of the building . . .*

this floor actually looks quite nice. Certainly more modern than the FBI headquarters with its carpet from 1985.

"I'm Sean O'Hara – we spoke on the phone," the older gentleman said. "And this is my assistant, Tony D'Amato."

Reagan smiled and shook hands with them both, having to fight the urge to wipe her palm on her pant leg after coming in contact with Tony's extremely sweaty skin. *Is he always sweaty or is he nervous about something?* she wondered before speaking. "Thank you both for staying late tonight to meet with me."

"Not a problem," Mr. O'Hara replied. "What can we do for you?"

The FBI agent smiled again and took a breath to compose herself before launching into her cover story – another half-truth that she wasn't proud of. "As you know, I work for the FBI. I was assigned to investigate possible weak spots in our nation's medical security."

"Medical security?" sweaty Tony asked.

Reagan nodded her head affirmatively. "You never know which areas criminals or terrorists might try to hit next. So I basically just want to take a look around, and maybe you can tell me what kind of procedures you have in place to make sure the blood supply is secure."

"Absolutely," said the Irishman. Turning to his Italian assistant, O'Hara added: "Tony here handles a lot more intake than I do – I'm usually in the back sorting and setting up distributions – so he'd probably be better at explaining that side of things."

"Okay," Reagan agreed, also turning her focus to Tony, who she had now concluded was really just that sweaty all of the time.

"Shooah," Tony said with a grin. It was very obvious to both his boss and Reagan that he liked the look of this tall, skinny strawberry blonde. "There's a lot goin' on in the day, but we always have somebody up heeah to meet people as they come in." Reaching over to the desk beside him, Tony picked up a clipboard with blank white forms on it. "Everyone droppin' off blood fills out one of these forms heeah," he went on, handing the clipboard to Reagan, "an' then we cawl to the back an' somebody comes up to get the blood. Beforrah we take the blood, though, we check an' make shooah the person put on the fooum checks out. Address, date of blood drive . . . all of that."

Reagan was furiously scribbling in her notebook trying to keep up with the rapid speech and strong accent of the Red Cross worker. "Okay," she said, "and is the blood ever left unattended?"

"Nevuh."

"I assume you follow that procedure for every donation?" Reagan asked.

"Ev'ry one," Tony answered.

"No exceptions?"

"None on my watch," he said assuredly. "An' I'm heeah ev'ry day."

"Good," responded Reagan with a smile. "Now, Mr. O'Hara, if you wouldn't mind showing me your side of things? How exactly does a regional blood distribution center work anyway?"

"I'm glad you asked," the friendly, non-sweaty Sean replied. "Follow me – I'll talk as we walk."

The three people started down a hallway with a wall on one side and rows of portable cubicles on the other. "We receive blood from local blood drives and from smaller Red Cross banks around the region. Once the blood gets here," the man explained, "we test it for various kinds of diseases, bacteria, or really anything that would make it unfit for patient use."

O'Hara paused as he unlocked a set of doors with his keys, and Reagan noted how much more she liked the manager than the assistant manager. For starters, Mr. O'Hara wasn't ogling her like she was a piece of fresh meat. Secondly, he didn't have anywhere near the level of

New York accent that Tony did. And third – well, third went back to first because the way the assistant manager kept staring at Reagan's lady parts was really creeping her out.

"There we go," O'Hara said as the doors unlocked and Reagan and Tony followed him inside the laboratory/warehouse.

"Why isn't the blood tested closer to where it's donated? Why does it all have to come here?" asked Agent White.

"Good question. A couple of reasons, actually. First is cost: the Red Cross doesn't have enough money to buy any more of the equipment or hire the kind of staff necessary to conduct all of the screening tests that we do. And second relates to distribution needs: hospitals need access to certain amounts of every blood type, but what they need isn't always available in their immediate area. Because we sort the blood we get by type, we're able to send hospitals exactly what they need."

Reagan wrote a few more lines in her notebook and looked up. "I think I've got it. So the big regional centers like this one have stockpiles of Type A, Type B, etcetera, and then hospitals can call up and say 'we're running low on X type of blood.'"

"Exactly," the manager responded.

"Okay," she said, nodding. "Just two more quick questions and then I'll get out of here so you gentlemen can go home. First, Tony, do you know if every distribution center follows those same intake procedures?"

"They should," answered Tony. "We go through trainin' when we staht work heeah, and that fooum is the same ev'rywheyah."

"And I guess either one of you can answer this: where are all of the distribution centers located?"

Sean O'Hara was the first to respond. "It's done by region. We handle the upper mid-Atlantic and New

England. There's one for the Southeast in Nashville, Tennessee. Midwest is in Chicago. And then there's one in I think Denver and maybe Los Angeles too."

"Awesome," Reagan said, and she meant it. Despite its scary beginning, this visit had been very productive. She now felt much better about the security of the blood supply, which also meant that she felt a lot more confident in thinking that this whole virus poisoning theory was incorrect.

TWENTY-NINE

Approximately an hour and a half north of the New York City Red Cross facility, factoring in the traffic on the Hutchinson River Parkway and Reagan getting lost twice trying to get out of Queens, lay the tony bedroom community of Rye, NY. The kind of place where investment bankers and their society wives might move when they decided to have kids. Which, according to the file Reagan read earlier that day, was exactly the kind of situation that she was facing with this next patient's family. Ramiro and Elena Hernandez had grown up in the same San Antonio neighborhood – he was her older brother's best friend – and they managed to stay together through college and his meteoric rise up the ranks of the notoriously cutthroat banking industry. The couple had just moved from Manhattan to the suburbs a year ago. Mrs. Hernandez's medical file mentioned something about a miscarriage.

Reagan couldn't help but gape in awe at the size and beauty of the houses on the perfectly manicured, tree-lined street where the Hernandez family lived. It was like something straight out of Norman Rockwell, except richer. *So this is how the other half lives*, Reagan mused as she pulled her rickety yet serviceable rental car into the Hernandez's driveway. She noticed that there were several other cars parked near the house as well – probably family members who were still in town after the funeral.

Once again Agent White did her trademark shoulder shake to calm her nerves as she made her way up the sidewalk to the front door. It was just past eight pm, which meant Reagan was on time . . . she had told Mr. Hernandez via email that he could expect her between eight and eight-thirty.

The decorative glass front door swung open before Reagan had a chance to knock. A startlingly handsome man in a perfectly-tailored suit, sans jacket and with a loosened tie, stood in the open doorway. He was tall, dark, and gorgeous, Reagan readily admitted before reminding herself not to stare at the man. *He's a widower. He's the victim's husband. Pull yourself together.*

The man's deep voice pulled Reagan back to the present. "Agent White, I presume?"

She nodded her head and replied "yes" while suddenly feeling very self-conscious about the shabby, wrinkled state of her black pantsuit.

Unaware of his visitor's thoughts, the man stepped back and motioned for Reagan to come inside. "Sorry for springing the door open on you like that. My sister's baby is asleep upstairs and I didn't want the doorbell to wake him up."

"Oh, not a problem," Reagan said with a slight smile. This was still a house in mourning – it wouldn't have been appropriate to give a full smile.

"Ramiro, ¿quién es?" an elderly woman called out from the living room.

"Nadie, Abuela. No te preocupes," the widower responded, surprising Reagan with how quickly he was able to switch back and forth between English and Spanish.

"Sorry about that," he apologized again. "My grandmother was just asking who I was talking to."

"Don't worry about it. I'm sorry to intrude like this. I was just up in the New York area doing another interview and I thought I would save a trip."

"Where are you coming from again?" Ramiro asked as he led Reagan into what appeared to be a home office or study of sorts. "Please, have a seat."

"D.C.," the agent responded.

"And you want to talk to me about Elena?"

"Yes sir, I do. If you don't mind." It struck Reagan as interesting that the only time Mr. Hernandez had any trace of a Spanish accent was when he spoke his wife's name.

"I wouldn't have agreed to this meeting if I wasn't okay with it," he replied, but without the bitter tone that would usually accompany a statement like that.

"Right, of course," Reagan said. She pulled her notepad and pen from her ever-present briefcase and started asking the same series of questions that she had asked Mike Russell's wife a few days earlier.

"As a bit of background, like I explained in my email, the Department of Health and Human Services flagged your wife as a possible victim of the deadly supervirus that has been hitting people across the country. I just have a few questions to ask about her illness."

"Okay," Ramiro said as he exhaled deeply. The pain he was experiencing was now clearly evident on his face as Reagan mentioned his late wife.

"Did Mrs. Hernandez travel anywhere recently?"

Ramiro shook his head. "No." And then: "she was six months pregnant. She didn't want to travel or do anything that could possibly endanger the baby." The grieving husband blinked his eyes rapidly in a desperate attempt to not cry.

"I'm so sorry for your loss," Reagan said gently, and she sincerely meant it. This man hadn't just lost his wife – he lost his baby too.

"Thank you," he answered, pulling a handkerchief from his pants pocket and wiping away the tears that he had been unable to avoid. "Let's continue with the questions. I don't want to keep my relatives waiting much longer."

"Certainly. Do you know of anyone else who died recently under similar circumstances?"

"Not personally," answered Mr. Hernandez. "I heard something on the news about a baby on Long Island who was suspected to have the same virus, but I don't know him or his family."

"Okay," Reagan said, making a note of his answer. "Have you or anyone else who had close contact with your wife travelled anywhere recently?"

"How recently?" asked Ramiro.

"Umm . . . the last three months." Reagan had no idea if that was the correct timeframe – she just threw out a guess.

"No," he replied, shaking his head. "I went to Sydney, Australia seven months ago, but that's it."

Agent White made a note of the Australia trip anyway. "Last one and then I'll get out of your hair. I know your wife was originally in the hospital because of a miscarriage . . . did you ever notice anyone suspicious hanging around?"

"You think somebody gave Elena the virus on purpose?" Unlike the rather sheltered Mrs. Russell, Reagan knew that it would be hard to get anything past Ramiro Hernandez. Taking a deep breath, she tried anyway.

"I'm just supposed to cover all of my bases. I wouldn't be a good FBI agent if I didn't see bad guys lurking around every corner."

The widower seemed to think about Reagan's answer for a minute before nodding his head. "I suppose not. And no, I don't remember seeing anyone suspicious."

Reagan clicked her pen shut and flipped her notebook closed. "Those are all of the questions I have for you. Again, thank you so much for agreeing to speak with me, and I'm very sorry for your loss."

"You're welcome. And thank you. Elena and the baby were both very special."

On that somber note, Reagan left the Hernandez's beautiful two-story home and began her journey back to her one-bedroom walk-up in Washington, DC.

THIRTY

Generally unconcerned with the investigation of their FBI counterpart, the six immunology experts comprising the President's task force continued to report to work every day at the NIH campus in Bethesda. It was frustrating work that still had no end in sight, since every failed test or experiment only served to add more time to their project and more patients to their list. Despite that, the doctors had managed to create a friendly, talkative work environment.

"Did y'all hear about that body they found in the national park?" Dr. Pingrey asked one Friday morning. Gill's question, phrased in his distinct Southern drawl, gave the appearance that the task force members were actually just old friends gossiping in the town square rather than medical superstars battling a killer virus. Gill liked to talk while he worked.

"You mean the one of the little girl?" Keri asked. She had seen something about it last night on the evening news but hadn't been paying much attention.

"Yeah," Gill replied affirmatively as he rummaged through a drawer of measuring utensils to find the one he needed.

Anthony had gone out to dinner with his wife Angela the night before and hadn't seen the local newscast. "What are you talking about?" The older gentleman wasn't usually one to gossip or make idle chit-chat while he worked, but the group's younger members had a talkative nature that had started to rub off on him.

"People found a little girl's body in Blue Mountain National Park yesterday," Keri answered. "They said it had probably been there a couple of months."

Leah had also heard bits and pieces of the news report. "Have they said yet who they think it is?"

Gill shook his head. "I don't think so. It's totally freaky, though."

"What's totally freaky?" Isaac asked as he walked into the lab where the rest of the team was working.

"That body they found yesterday," answered Gill. "All of her blood had been drained out."

Isaac's face turned to one of grossed-out disgust. "What in the world are you talking about?" Like Dr. Russo, Isaac didn't see any news the night before. He had been working there at the lab until very late.

Keri filled in her boss on the details. "Someone found the body of a little girl in Blue Mountain National Park. Like Gill said, all of her blood was missing from her body."

Isaac shook his head. "That is weird. Or what was the word you used, Gill?"

"Freaky."

"Yeah, very freaky," Isaac said. "It's probably some punk teenagers who read too many of those damn vampire books."

"You know who I think it is?" Leah joined in. "I bet it's that girl who went missing a couple of months ago." She turned to Anthony. "Remember, we talked about it when it happened? It was all over the news."

"Oh yeah," Anthony nodded his head. "Gill and David, you might not have heard about it since you were down in Atlanta. A schoolgirl told her parents she was going out to play one afternoon and never came home. I think they found some of her stuff in a dumpster in downtown Baltimore, but the trail went cold after that."

"I remember seeing all of the flyers that her family put up when she went missing," Keri commented. "Poor little thing."

"That's so sad," David added. "Maybe it is her. If it was one of my kids, I'd at least want to be able to have that closure and give her a proper burial."

Everyone in the room nodded in agreement with David's statement as they went back to work. For her parents' sake, if the girl wasn't alive, they hoped the police had at least found her body.

****

Despite it being the weekend, the sun fell and rose and would've started to fall again without Isaac's notice if not for the growling in his stomach alerting him that he hadn't eaten in over half a day. Absorbed in his work, Isaac ignored the low grumble at first but, not liking being ignored, his stomach quickly progressed to a full-throated roar and added a splash of light-headedness just to make sure it got its neglectful owner's attention.

Realizing that he probably did need to eat something and maybe take a quick power nap, Isaac finally rose from his chair and walked over to his desk. Picking up his cell phone, Isaac stared in disbelief as the little neon numbers on the screen told him that he had been working for fifteen hours straight. Sure, there was the occasional call of nature, but with a half-bath attached directly to his office, Isaac literally hadn't left that room since eight o'clock the night before. And it was nearing noon now.

Isaac shook his head and lightly slapped himself across the face in an effort to wake up. *You're of no good to anyone if your brain can't function right*, the doctor thought. Except that was the crazy thing about his all-nighter. Despite being exhausted at the end of another long workweek, despite malnutrition brought on by too many microwaved dinners and not enough fruits and vegetables, despite the inevitable burnout creeping in as the task force completed its fourth week of battle with the deadly virus . . . despite all of that, Isaac had made incredible progress in the past several hours.

Using mostly the genetic sequencing PCR technique, Isaac had been able to identify some of the genes that were combining to express the virus' deadly proteins. He wasn't finished yet – not by a long shot – but he was making progress. Pretty soon he might even be able to proceed to the next phase of running tests on an animal model to see if they worked. Once he identified more of the viral contents, Isaac also planned to employ reverse genetic approaches that would, in essence, purposely mutate different genes to see if he could mimic the illness in animals. Despite several long weeks of darkness, Isaac was finally beginning to see light at the end of the tunnel.

The doctor actually found himself smiling as he strolled through the third floor's whitewashed hallways toward the small break room in one corner of the building. It was empty, as no one aside from Isaac made a habit of being there at all hours on a Saturday. *We should probably paint these walls*, Isaac thought. *Or at least put up some pictures. This place is dreary.* Even with those thoughts, he continued to smile as he opened the community refrigerator and scanned its contents for something edible. All of the Tupperware containers were clearly marked with the name of the person who had brought the food, but Isaac didn't care about that as he picked up a small dish containing what looked like pasta with Alfredo sauce and took it over to the microwave. "Anthony Russo," he said aloud, reading the name of the pasta's owner. Isaac shrugged his shoulders and hit the start button to reheat the food. "Shouldn't have left it behind."

Fifteen minutes later, with a full stomach and heavy eyelids, Isaac pushed shut the door to his office and fell face first onto the black leather couch pushed up against one of the walls. "Nap time," he sighed contentedly before drifting off to sleep.

THIRTY-ONE

Two days after Isaac's solitary sleepover at the NIH, Reagan White yawned widely at her own desk in the FBI headquarters. A big yawn – the kind where your eyes close and your chest and arms inevitably swell upwards. There was no doubt about it: she was exhausted. The drive from the Hernandez's home in Rye back to LaGuardia airport had seemed to take forever, then her plane was delayed; all of which combined to keep Reagan from getting home until 1:30am. Reagan's work on the virus had been temporarily halted to help with the investigation around the body found in the national park, meaning that she still hadn't recuperated from her New York travels. And now it was eight am on a Monday and she was staring at the same stack of medical files that she had been on her desk for well over a week. *This is the worst wild goose chase ever*, she thought with a sigh.

Reagan checked her watch again. At the top of her priority list for the day was a phone call to Maureen McDougall, the sister of yet another suspected victim of the virus. Maureen's sister, Lisa Masters, was forty-years-old and in the hospital for breast cancer treatments when she developed her mysterious new symptoms. And while a day trip to New York was easy enough to get approved, there was no way Reagan could convince her boss to pay for a flight out to Arizona where Maureen and Lisa lived. So she would have to settle for a phone call.

"Eight a.m.," Reagan said aloud, "which means it's only six in Phoenix. So I need to wait at least three hours before I call out there." She glared again at the papers covering the whole of her disorganized desk. "Hospitals," Reagan finally said with resignation. "I need to check with all of the hospitals to make sure there aren't any irregularities with the visitors to the blood banks."

****

Three and a half hours and four and a half cups of coffee later, Reagan was almost ready to pull her hair out. The hospitals she contacted were happy to scan and email her copies of visitor logs from the approximate times when the patients were infected, but staring at meaningless names and purpose-of-visit codes for hours on end was enough to make a person go crazy.

Reagan closed her eyes and shook her head vigorously back and forth in an attempt to wake up. Once again, she checked the clock. "Eleven thirty. Finally!" The agent quickly brushed aside the visitor logs to find Lisa Masters' case file. "Here we go. Next of kin: Maureen McDougall, sister. Hmm," Reagan said pensively. "McDougall must be a married name." She then reached across her desk and picked up the phone. "Alright, Maureen, let's see what you have to say."

****

Maureen Masters McDougall answered her cell phone on the third ring. An interior designer by trade, she always left her phone on in case a client needed to reach her. "McDougall Designs, this is Maureen speaking."

"Hi Mrs. McDougall," an unfamiliar voice said through the phone. "My name is Reagan White; I'm an agent with the FBI."

Reagan heard the woman gasp. "Oh my gosh, are my kids okay?"

"Yes, yes they're fine," Reagan assured her.

"And my husband?"

"Him too. Listen, ma'am," the agent quickly said to keep Maureen from interrupting again, "I'm calling in regard to your sister, Lisa Masters."

"Lisa's dead," her sister said curtly.

"Yes ma'am, I know. And I'm very sorry for your loss. I'm calling because we suspect –"

"Who is 'we'?" Maureen cut in again.

"The FBI and the Department of Health and Human Services," Reagan answered matter-of-factly. She could already tell that this interview was going to be much more challenging than the other two.

"Okay. Go on," said the bossy woman.

Agent White took it all in stride. She had dealt with people like Mrs. McDougall before. "We suspect that your sister might have contracted a rare virus that has been claiming lives across the country."

There was a pause on the other end of the line. "You mean that SuperAIDS thing?"

"Yes," Reagan replied. "If it's alright, I would like to ask you a few questions, since you're her next of kin."

"Okay," Maureen said quietly, obviously shocked by the revelation that it might have been a mysterious virus that killed her sister.

As with the previous interviews, Reagan grabbed her notepad and pen before asking her first question.

"Had your sister travelled anywhere recently?"

"No," answered Maureen. "The cancer made her too weak to travel."

"Right. Of course. Have you or anyone else who came in contact with Ms. Masters travelled anywhere recently?"

"Umm . . . I go to Los Angeles once a month for business. But I don't know of any exotic travel or anything like that, unless one of her doctors had."

Reagan made a note to check the international travel history of the medical staff who treated affected patients. There could be something there.

"I think Los Angeles is fine," Agent White said reassuringly. "I just have a couple more questions. Did your sister or do you personally know of anyone else who has died recently under similar conditions?"

"You're looking for a Patient Zero, aren't you?" Maureen asked. "I've seen those movies. Mysterious illness, people dying, and in the end they always trace it back to the weird guy who thought it would be cool to bring a wild monkey home from Africa."

Reagan tried not to laugh at the other woman's depiction. "I'm just trying to ask a few questions, ma'am."

"Well, the answer is no. I don't know anyone else who checked into the hospital for chemo treatments and died three and a half weeks later of a fever, vomiting, skin boils, and massive organ failure."

Reagan winced at the description. "I'm so sorry for your loss."

"Thank you," Mrs. McDougall replied. "Any more questions?"

"Yes ma'am, just one more. Do you ever remember seeing anyone suspicious hanging around the hospital?"

The other woman snorted into the phone. "I've seen that movie too. A deranged madman disguises himself as a doctor and goes around killing patients in hospitals. You people really have no clue what you're looking for, do you?"

"We're currently considering all options," Reagan answered, putting bureaucratic spin on the situation.

"Same difference," Maureen said sharply. "No, I didn't see anyone suspicious. Now if we're done I have work to do."

"Yes, of course. Thank you for your time."

****

Almost immediately after hanging up with the victim's sister in Arizona, a man's gruff voice barked at Reagan from the doorway to her office. "Alright White. You've had almost two weeks. Whatcha got?"

Her boss' sudden appearance in her office startled Reagan. *Some of the higher ups must be riding him hard for an update*, she thought. *He never comes to my office.*

Motioning to a chair on the other side of her desk, Reagan replied: "Mr. Assistant Deputy Director, please have a seat."

The grizzled veteran shut the room's door and then took the chair offered to him. "So?" he asked impatiently.

Reagan wasted no time with her response. "I've read through all of the patient files multiple times. I've interviewed the doctor in charge of the task force that's working on this same case. I've talked with several different families who lost a loved one to the disease, and I even went to the Red Cross' giant blood distribution warehouse in New York."

"And?"

"I don't think it's terrorism," she answered bluntly.

"Why not?"

"It just doesn't seem possible. It would literally take a medical and tactical genius to pull off a mass poisoning like this."

The agent's boss looked at her skeptically. "Such geniuses do exist."

Reagan sighed heavily. "I know, but they're very rare." Taking another deep breath, she tried to explain her reasoning in a way that would convince her boss that she was right. "Tactically, the easiest part of the scheme would be creating the virus," she began. "According to this Dr. Carlson guy, people make up new viruses all the time for experiments and therapy and stuff like that. So let's just say we've got a madman and he makes the virus. It's delivered through the bloodstream, so now he has to find a way to get this bad blood into the patients' bodies."

"He can just sneak into a hospital," Bruce Molina hypothesized.

"And if all of the patients were from the same hospital or even the same couple of hospitals, I'd agree with you," Reagan replied. "But they're not. They're from all over the country. And," she added, wanting to preempt his next objection, "I checked visitor logs and any blood bank abnormalities at all of the hospitals that have reported infected patients. It's all clean."

Assistant Deputy Director Molina breathed deeply and leaned back in his seat. "So you're telling me I can report to my superiors that, in your professional opinion, there has not been an intentional attack on America's blood supply."

Reagan nodded her head vigorously. "Yes."

"Okay," the older man said as he put his hands on his knees and stood up. "But if you're wrong, it's your ass on the line. Not mine."

"Understood, sir."

THIRTY-TWO

Just up the road from Reagan in Bethesda, MD, four of the six task force doctors were seated around the table in Conference Room D. "How many new cases have been reported since the last time we did a recap?" Keri asked. She was doing her best to appear confident and authoritative since she was in charge of this morning's task force meeting.

"Where's Isaac?" Gill asked, starting off the day with his usual extra-large cup of triple-shot coffee. Keri didn't know how his veins didn't explode with all of the caffeine charging through them.

Keri gave a small smile and then answered: "Drs. Carlson and Malhotra are at a meeting at the White House. Isaac told me last night that we should have our Monday morning session like always and that I should run things."

Gill, who had grown to see Keri as a threat for future research fellowship grants, obviously didn't like her answer but didn't appear willing to challenge Isaac's instructions either.

Sensing victory, Keri repeated, "how many new cases?"

Dr. Russo was the first one to answer. With the two senior members of the task force gone, Anthony's age made him a natural leader in the room. "Leah," Anthony asked, "can you add these to the board?" Keri knew that Dr. Mann had to be getting frustrated with her role as group secretary, but when it came down to it, the girl had nice handwriting and was the most junior of the task force members. *Sucks being the rookie sometimes*, Keri mused.

"Okay," Leah said as she took her position at the side of the room. "I'm ready. Get us caught up."

The boisterous Italian grandfather grabbed a stack of patient files from the center of the table and slid them over in front of him. "We have six more patients that we haven't talked about yet," Anthony began. "First up is Alicia Kendrick. Thirty-three from Philadelphia. Admitted to Temple's burn unit after a grease fire gave her third degree burns on seventy percent of her body." Anthony paused as grimaces from the other doctors filled the room.

"Sorry to interrupt, Anthony," Keri said, "but Isaac and I went up to Philly to see this patient. Eight days after the fire, she started showing symptoms of our disease and was moved to an isolation room. Unlike a lot of the other patients, she wasn't battling any immune system problems so her body has been able to fight back more."

"*Was* able to fight back more," Anthony corrected. "Ms. Kendrick died yesterday. Three and a half weeks post-transfusion."

The other doctors in the room could see the sadness that struck Keri's face when Anthony said that the patient had died. It was one thing to read their files or see their pictures up on the whiteboard, but Dr. Dupree had met this woman. Talked with her. Seen the disease first hand.

Ugh, Keri thought as she fought to keep back a tear. *Isaac is right. I do get too emotionally involved with my patients*. Wiping under her eyes, Keri then motioned toward the pile of patient files still untouched on the conference table. "Keep going. We don't have all day."

Anthony Russo quickly put Ms. Kendrick's file to the side and picked up the next one from the stack in front of him. "Here we go. Marcus Johnson from Tennessee. He was twenty-one years old. Tore several knee ligaments playing soccer and had to have reconstructive surgery. Complications during surgery resulted in him needing to have a blood transfusion. Marcus presented with a fever, cough, joint pain, and diarrhea six days after surgery." Dr. Russo took a breath and then concluded: "He died of kidney failure sixteen days after that."

"Next?" Leah asked as she finished filling in Marcus Johnson's spot on the whiteboard chart.

"Holly Steinberger. Sixty-two from Akron, Ohio. She was already in the hospital waiting on a liver transplant. Chart notes say cirrhosis due to alcoholism." Anthony ran a hand through his hair and then flipped through a few pages of the Steinberger file to find the rest of the patient's pertinent information. "Holly died of multiple organ failure, starting with the liver, ten days after the suspected tainted transfusion."

"Ten days?" Keri exclaimed. "Only three days post-incubation period?"

Dr. Russo nodded his head up and down in confirmation. "I guess her body was too weak to fight it."

"This virus is a bitch," Gill said, and for once Keri agreed with him.

Dr. Dupree then glanced down at her wristwatch and, noting the time, said: "give us the next three really quickly. Name, age, and timespan. Then we need to get to work. Leah, you can stay a few minutes after and finish filling in the chart."

"Okay," Anthony agreed. "Jane Lambert, sixty-four, colon cancer. Died seventeen days post-transfusion. John Martinez, fifty-six, lung transplant. Died twenty-two days post-transfusion. And last but not least," he said, picking up the bottom file, "Teresa Lewis, twenty-eight, parasite. Eww. Sorry . . . uh . . . Ms. Lewis died eighteen days post-transfusion."

When Dr. Russo finished speaking, Keri placed her hands on the wooden table and rose to stand, the same way she had seen her boss do a thousand times before. It was Isaac's tell-tale signal that the meeting was over, and Keri had adopted it without even thinking. "Alright," she said. "Isaac and David should be back within an hour or so. In the meantime, let's get to work."

THIRTY-THREE

David Malhotra looked nervous as he and Dr. Carlson made their way from the Northwest Appointment Gate to the West Wing of the White House. Isaac wasn't nervous, though. Sure, he was about to be meeting with the leader of the free world, but Isaac was the one with the information. He didn't want anything from President Hughes; the president wanted something from him. *So what's to be nervous about?* Isaac thought as he strode confidently toward the Marine-guarded entryway.

****

Okay, maybe a few butterflies snuck their way into my stomach, Isaac admitted to himself as he and David sat just outside of the Oval Office waiting for their turn to meet with President Richard Hughes. *No shame in that. He is the president, after all.* The door beside Isaac opened and he immediately jumped to attention with his colleague quickly following suit.

"Well don't just stand there, come on in," the man who opened the door declared as he waved the two doctors inside. "Now I don't think I've officially met either of you," the gray-haired, clean-shaven, extremely overweight man continued. "Dr. Carlson, I've talked to you before on the phone, but let's do the hand shake anyway. Daniel Bader, White House Chief of Staff," he said, sticking out his hand toward Isaac.

It was a firm grip, almost too firm in Isaac's opinion, but the jovial Chief of Staff was also a very large man so the strong handshake didn't surprise the doctor much. *He must be nearly three hundred pounds*, the rail thin Dr. Carlson thought to himself. *And with the kind of stress he deals with on a daily basis? His cardiologist must absolutely hate him.*

President Richard Hughes' booming voice woke Isaac from his thoughts. "Dr. Carlson. Dr. Malhotra. Have you got this thing solved yet?"

David, Daniel, and Isaac finished shaking hands as the president gestured for them all to sit down on the two parallel couches in the middle of the world's most famous oval.

"Not yet, sir," Isaac responded. "But we're making progress."

"Fill me in," said President Hughes, leaning back into the couch and crossing one leg over the other. "How many people is it now?"

"Fifteen," David answered.

"That's correct," Isaac continued. "So far we have fifteen identified cases. The numbers have spiked within the last week, but that's because we had the CDC issue an alert to every hospital telling them to report any suspected cases to us."

"And that alert is what has my Press Secretary fielding questions left and right about an 'outbreak,'" the president commented, using his fingers to put air quotes around the word outbreak.

"Yes sir, I'm afraid so," responded Isaac. "But we really felt like –"

"I'm sorry to interrupt," David said worriedly, "but are you feeling alright, Mr. Bader?"

Dr. Carlson and President Hughes immediately turned to look at the Chief of Staff who, in a matter of minutes, had gone from comfortable and focused to sweaty, red-faced, and dazed.

"I – I – I don't know," Daniel struggled to answer. "I feel like . . . AHHHHH!"

The powerful man screamed in pain as he clutched his left arm and collapsed off the edge of the couch onto the floor.

"He's having a heart attack," David calmly said in a way only a doctor could. "Have someone call an ambulance – or whatever you do at the White House. And I'm sure there's a defibrillator somewhere nearby."

The Commander-in-Chief followed orders perfectly as he ran out of his office and yelled for his doctor, an ambulance, and the little red box that just might be able to shock his best friend's heart back to life.

****

Against the advice and warnings of the Secret Service, President Hughes rode in the ambulance with his Chief of Staff on its way to George Washington Hospital. With the sirens, flashing lights, and accompanying motorcade, less than ten minutes passed between Daniel's collapse in the Oval Office and his arrival in the emergency room. Drs. Carlson and Malhotra had been swept up in the panic that overtook the West Wing and somehow found themselves in the back of a black Secret Service SUV being driven to the hospital as part of the motorcade.

"I realize they probably keep a doctor in the White House at all times," David began, his hushed tone unnecessary yet fitting given the situation, "but they had him in the ambulance literally in like two minutes."

Isaac nodded his head. "The ambulance is always there too. Although I doubt they would've let the janitor use it if he was the one who had the heart attack."

David huffed in agreement. "No joke. I can't believe Hughes went with him, though."

"I understand that more than I understand us joining in the motorcade."

"Well, yeah," David replied.

The two men ended their brief conversation as the presidential motorcade careened into the emergency room parking lot. The doctors quickly exited their car and rushed to catch up to the president, not wanting to be left behind when the Secret Service inevitably whisked him away to a private, secure room.

****

Richard Hughes hadn't been this worried since his wife had an emergency Caesarean section with their second child. That was twenty-one years ago, and the memories of that night came flooding back as he once again found himself pacing the floor of a hospital waiting room, his palms sweaty and his stomach in knots.

Daniel Bader was his best friend. Had been ever since they met sophomore year of college just down the road at Georgetown. Richard was the jock, the bro, the member of the club lacrosse team known as much for its off-field antics as its on-field ones. Daniel, on the other hand, had nerdy Capitol Hill intern written all over him. He was already getting chubby from too many campaign donuts, and was as loud and boisterous as one would expect someone who grew up on the Jersey Shore to be. But Daniel and the mild-mannered teacher's son from Arizona had hit it off instantly when paired together for a project in a Presidential Politics class, and the two had been inseparable ever since.

After a few minutes, the leader of the free world finally realized that he wasn't alone in the room. He stopped pacing momentarily and looked around, noting a Secret Service agent (with three more stationed outside the door), his Deputy Chief of Staff, and the two doctors who had been briefing him on what sounded like an absolutely terrifying disease that caused people to die within three weeks of first showing symptoms.

"What are you two doing here?" the president bluntly asked, not realizing for a second that he had spoken aloud the question in his head.

For once Dr. Malhotra was glad that he wasn't the head of the task force, since right now he was able to defer answering the question over to Dr. Carlson.

"I guess we kind of got swept up in the rush of everything, sir," Isaac replied more than a little nervously. He was careful to say 'rush' and not 'excitement' so as to not provoke the already high-strung chief executive. "We can leave if you'd like." Isaac didn't really want to leave – he wanted to be in the middle of the action and find out if Mr. Bader would be okay – but he also didn't want to sit there in a creaky, cramped hospital chair only to serve as a verbal punching bag for Richard Hughes.

"No, no. Stay," the president ordered. "As long as you're here you might as well be useful. Distract me. Tell me more about your disease."

"Well, it isn't really *our* disease –" David began, causing Isaac to cringe and the president's eyes to flash.

"And I'm not really in the mood to play word games," President Hughes roared. "You're researching it, so it's your fucking disease. Now tell me about it."

David opened his mouth to begin again but the president cut him off. "Not you. You," he said, pointing to Isaac.

"Well, sir, we've been working to isolate the exact cause of the illness, which was difficult because there are many different symptoms and many different types of patients."

"Types of patients?" Hughes asked.

"Yes sir. Some illnesses target certain segments of the population more than others, making it easier to pinpoint the cause," Isaac explained. "But that hasn't been the case here. It seems everyone is fair game."

Just as Isaac finished his sentence, the emergency room's attending physician came through the door, followed closely by Daniel Bader's wife. President Hughes barely acknowledged the new doctor's presence as he rushed over and enveloped Emily Bader in a giant bear hug. "I'm so, so sorry Emily," Richard said, his words muffled by the woman's hair as he continued to hug her. "We got him here as soon as we could. And he's a fighter. He'll make it through this. Right, doctor?" the president asked, turning to the hospital surgeon for confirmation.

"He is a fighter," the doctor agreed, nodding his head. "But your husband is in pretty bad shape." Noticing the number of people in the room, he added, "maybe we can go somewhere and talk more privately?"

Emily shook her head violently no, so hard that her tears ran in zigzagged lines down her cheeks. "Just tell me." As the wife of the White House Chief of Staff, she was used to random people being in the room for all kinds of otherwise-private conversations. Plus she knew that the information would be all over the TV and internet soon enough anyway. There would be no keeping a lid on this story.

The cardiologist took a deep breath and then began. "Ma'am, your husband had a severe acute myocardial infarction. A heart attack," he clarified. "We have stabilized him for the time being, but he's going to need bypass surgery to repair the damage to his heart."

"Do it," Emily blurted out.

"I'm sorry?" the doctor answered, confused.

"Do the surgery. What are you waiting for? Go fix my husband."

President Hughes couldn't help but grin a little as he watched his best friend's wife issue orders like a drill sergeant. *Daniel might be one of the most powerful and intimidating men in Washington, but he's got nothing on his wife*, the president mused, his arm still wrapped around the woman's shoulders.

"Yes ma'am. We'll do the surgery. I just want to make you aware, though, that there are some risks –"

"Do the surgery," Mrs. Bader repeated.

George Washington Hospital's best surgeon was smart enough to know when to shut up and do as he was told. With a brief nod, he turned and left the room.

THIRTY-FOUR

After the door clicked shut behind the doctor tasked with saving Daniel Bader's life, Isaac took a step forward. "Excuse me, Mrs. Bader?" he said softly, not wanting to intrude on the situation too much but feeling compelled to speak.

Through sniffles and tears, the thin woman with close cropped, dyed red hair managed to pull herself away from her friend Richard's comforting embrace and turned to face the stranger talking to her.

"Yes?" she replied.

"My name is Dr. Isaac Carlson. This is my associate Dr. David Malhotra. We were in a meeting with your husband and President Hughes when Mr. Bader went into cardiac arrest."

Emily Bader simply stared back at Isaac, still not sure why he was in the room or talking to her. Sensing the woman's confusion, Isaac continued:

"There's something I want to make you aware of regarding your husband's surgery."

"Isaac –" David warned, seeing where Dr. Carlson was going with the conversation and not finding it necessary or productive.

"No," said Isaac dismissively, "she should hear it. If it was your spouse going into surgery, wouldn't you want to know?"

David grudgingly nodded his head yes and took a step backwards, giving Isaac the floor.

"What is it?" Daniel's wife asked, her voice full of equal parts curiosity and fear.

"It's what we planned on telling you at the White House, Mr. President, before –" Isaac paused, seeing Mrs. Bader cringe. "It's what we planned on telling you at the

White House," he corrected, leaving off the reference to Daniel's heart attack.

"So tell us," President Hughes said irritably, his patience run thin due to the stress of the past hour.

"We've been able to determine that the illness is a virus, and that the virus is being transmitted through infected blood."

"But how are the people coming in contact with the infected blood?" asked the president.

"Blood transfusions," David answered.

"Wait, hold on," Emily broke in, putting both of her arms and hands out in front of her in a 'stop' motion. "What are you talking about?"

Isaac and David looked to the president, but he simply gestured back to them. "Gentlemen," he said, his way of conveying that he wanted the two doctors to explain the situation.

Once again, Isaac took the lead.

"You may have heard on the news," the pathologist began, "or perhaps not, but there has been an illness affecting people in the United States for around a month now. President Hughes," Isaac said, gesturing toward the man as he referenced him, "and your husband organized a task force to investigate it. I'm the head of that task force, and Dr. Malhotra here is one of my top deputies."

Mrs. Bader shook her head in confusion. "I'm sorry, but what does any of this have to do with my husband?"

David joined in the conversation now. "Like Dr. Carlson said, we believe the virus is being spread through transfusions that have tainted blood." He paused for a second, and then delivered the blow. "Blood transfusions are fairly standard in heart bypass surgery."

The full weight of what Isaac and David were saying hit President Hughes first, since he was more familiar with the virus than Daniel's wife was. "Why the hell didn't you say something earlier?" he yelled. "You just let that doctor walk out of the room to go do an operation that might give Daniel AIDS?"

Mrs. Bader's eyes grew wide and she glared accusingly at the two doctors in the room. "What?!"

Isaac put his hands up in front of him defensively. "Just calm down for a second," he urged. "First of all, it's not AIDS. Just let me explain."

Neither President Hughes nor Emily Bader issued any reply, other than to fold their arms across their respective chests and raise their eyebrows in skeptical anticipation.

Isaac began by addressing Daniel's wife. "Your husband needed the bypass. He would die without it. There's nothing that I could've said earlier that would've changed that. I'm telling you about the blood transfusion risk now because I want you to be aware of what symptoms to watch for once he is released from the hospital."

"Couldn't you have told the other doctor, though?" Richard Hughes asked, not yet willing to give up his defense of his best friend. "Made him test the blood or something before they used it for his transfusion?"

"There's no test," David answered. "At least not yet." Turning to Mrs. Bader, he went on: "there really wasn't a choice to be made, ma'am. With the surgery, there's a chance he'll get the virus and die. Without the surgery, your husband would definitely die."

"You're telling me if he gets the bad blood then he'll definitely die?" Emily shrieked. "What kind of disease is this?"

"SuperAIDS," the president replied grimly. "Same symptoms, except you're dead within a couple of weeks."

The only woman in the room kept her fearful eyes trained on Isaac, pleading with him to tell her that the answer the friend who served as best man at her wedding had just given her was wrong. Unfortunately, all Isaac could do was sigh, lower his eyes, and nod his head in agreement. "More or less, yes, it is SuperAIDS."

Emily Bader responded by turning her back to the group, taking deep breaths in and out in an effort to regain her composure. After half a minute at the most, the mother of two turned back around, her eyes dry and her face serious. She looked only at Isaac.

"Have someone from your task force send over a copy of possible symptoms to watch for. In the meantime, you two need to leave. Go back to your office, or your lab, or wherever it is that this task force is working, and figure out how to cure this SuperAIDS." She waved dismissively toward the two men and then added: "you're of no use to anyone here."

THIRTY-FIVE

The front porch lights were on when Keri finally pulled into her driveway after another exhausting day at work. Today had been particularly rough since the two usual take-charge members of the task force, Isaac and David, had been gone the whole time. "I guess Scott beat me home," she said casually, referring to her husband of six years. "Then again, it is after eight o'clock," Keri added as she made her way up the sidewalk to their comfortable two-story stucco home. It was a little big for just two people, but one day there would be kids to fill the rooms. If Keri's husband had it his way, there would already be a little one running – or at least crawling – around.

Keri shook her head at the thought as she unlocked the door and walked inside. Scott was five years older than her, a partner in a prestigious DC law firm, and had wanted to start a family for years. Keri, on the other hand, knew that having kids would greatly impact her career. She wasn't the kind of person who could leave her child to be raised by a nanny, and there was no way she could ever get her own research lab while working kid-friendly hours. So Keri kept delaying, and Scott kept pushing, *and pretty soon we'll reach a boiling point*, she thought.

"Hey babe, how was your day?" Scott Dupree interrupted his wife's thoughts.

"Long," Keri sighed, kissing Scott hello. "Did you already eat?"

"Yeah, sorry. I was starving. I put some leftovers in the fridge for you though."

The doctor's grumbling stomach led her directly to the kitchen. Inside the large refrigerator, next to drawers of fruits and vegetables, was a Tupperware container full of freshly made chicken 'n' dumplings. Keri's stomach growled more loudly. "Mmm . . . my favorite."

"I know," Scott smiled proudly. The saying might be that the way to a man's heart was through his stomach, but after six years of marriage Scott knew that food was also the way to Keri Dupree's heart.

As wives often do when confronted by an unexpected gesture of kindness, Keri got suspicious. While her dinner was reheating in the microwave, she turned to face her six-foot-tall strong safety of a husband. "What happened?"

"What do you mean?" Scott was trying to feign innocence, but his wife didn't buy it.

"You beat me home from work, make my favorite dinner, and now that I look around I see that all of the dishes have also been washed, dried, and put away."

"Can't a husband just do something nice for his wife without facing the Spanish Inquisition?"

"No," Keri answered knowingly, folding her arms across her chest.

The beeping of the microwave interrupted the simmering disagreement between Mr. and Dr. Dupree. Scott hated when envelopes were addressed that way, even though it was correct. He thought it made them sound like a gay couple.

Keri, unwilling to let the conversation drop, sat down on a stool at the kitchen island to eat her food and asked again: "what happened?"

Her husband sighed. "I've been assigned a new case."

Keri glanced up from her plate with a quizzical look on her face. She could tell that the other shoe was yet to drop.

"I'm consulting on a multi-billion dollar trial," Scott continued. "In China."

The brunette doctor nearly choked on a dumpling. "China?"

Scott nodded. "Well, technically Hong Kong. I have to leave the day after tomorrow and will be gone at least a month."

Keri didn't reply. She just kept chewing her food and staring at her husband.

"Well, aren't you going to say anything?"

Finally, Keri nodded. "You say you want kids, but a father to young children can't just take off to foreign countries for months at a time."

Scott glared angrily at his wife. "The *only* reason I'm still assigned cases like this," he seethed, "is because I'm the only damn litigation partner who doesn't have children. So don't even try to throw that back at me right now."

Keri shoved her plate away from her and stood up. "Suddenly I'm not hungry anymore. I'm going to bed." She then turned on her heel and stalked out of the kitchen, but not before adding over her shoulder: "you can sleep on the couch."

****

Keri's co-workers weren't sure why she had been so moody for the several days since her fight with her husband, but they were all hoping she would snap out of it soon. The normally smiling and friendly Keri acted as a counterweight to Isaac's grumpy personality, but the quiet haze that had settled over her this week only served to make the mood on the third floor worse.

There was none of the usual chatter in the research lab this Wednesday morning, as Keri, David, and Isaac worked on a blood test while the rest of the team worked in another lab down the hall. The silence was interrupted by the arrival of the building's receptionist, Lois.

"Dr. Carlson, Dr. Malhotra, Dr. Dupree, there's someone here to see you."

The tears that the front desk clerk had recently shed were audible in the woman's voice as she stood in the doorway of the lab where the three doctors were working to create a test to screen for the virus that continued to kill people around the country.

"We're kind of in the middle of something here, Lois," Isaac responded, barely looking up from his microscope.

"I know that, and I'm sorry to interrupt. It's just that –" the middle aged receptionist paused mid-sentence to blow her nose as the tears returned.

"Who is it?" asked Keri. Everyone in the building knew how important these doctors' work was, so this woman clearly wouldn't have bothered them if not for something important.

"It's the Simanskis," Lois answered. "They drove down from Long Island to see you."

"Simanski . . ." Isaac said, trying to place the name. He had so many patients and new staffers that it was getting hard to keep everyone straight. Anguish washed over his face as Isaac figured it out. "Simanski. Cooper Simanski. Male, eight days old, hospitalized after being born prematurely."

Drs. Malhotra and Dupree looked up from their microscopes and put down their slides as they heard Isaac describe one of the recent victims of the virus.

"His family is here?" Keri asked as tears began to well in her eyes too.

"Mmm hmm," the receptionist answered affirmatively. "I took them into a conference room on the first floor instead of the one you have been using during the task force meetings, since the whiteboard in there had patient information all over it."

"Thank you, Lois. We'll be right down," Isaac said as he stood up from the stool he had been sitting on and walked over to his desk to get little Cooper's file. He then followed David and Keri out of the room.

****

The first thing that struck Keri Dupree as she entered the conference room was how young the Simanskis were. Keri's husband kept telling her that they needed to have children before they got too old, but the devastated husband and wife sitting in front of Keri now were younger than she was. Thirty years old at the most. Thirty years old with a dead baby boy.

Her boss' words brought Keri back to the present.

"Mr. and Mrs. Simanski, I'm Dr. Isaac Carlson." Isaac extended his arm to shake hands with the two visitors as he continued introductions. "These are two of the doctors helping me on this case, David Malhotra from the Centers for Disease Control and Keri Dupree from here at the NIH."

All five adults took turns shaking hands and then sat down together at one end of the large conference table.

"We're so sorry for your loss," Isaac said softly but with conviction. Once again, Keri was amazed at how well her boss could turn on the charm when he needed to. She also got the feeling, though, that little Cooper's death had indeed struck Isaac harder than the other patients. *Heck, who am I kidding? It struck us all harder.*

Cooper's dad placed one arm around his wife's shoulders and used his free hand to hold the hand of the grieving mother. Taking a deep breath, frantically blinking his eyes in a desperate attempt to keep from crying, Bernie Simanski finally spoke.

"I know you are really busy with other patients and trying to solve this thing, and I know it probably doesn't help matters to have us come down here and interrupt your work. But, even though Cooper was only with us for eight days, he is still our son and we just – we want you to know what you're fighting for. We want you to know Cooper beyond just some numbers on a chart."

David was the first one to pull himself together enough to respond. "Of course. I have two children back home in

Atlanta and I would be doing the same thing as you if this happened to one of them."

Comforted by David's words, the New York City firefighter continued: "We brought you some pictures. I know he's covered in tubes and stuff, but even with all that he's still just the cutest little guy in the world."

Isaac noticed that Mr. Simanski hadn't yet been able to bring himself to speak of his son in the past tense.

"He has blue eyes," Laura Simanski chimed in, sniffling back tears as she spoke. "The prettiest blue eyes." Sniffles turned into sobs and Bernie pulled his wife in closer to him. "Bernie and I both have brown eyes," Laura went on, "but my dad had blue eyes. The same color blue as Coop. We thought that – that – " her story broke off as the flood of tears that the young mother had been holding back finally broke the dam and rushed down her face.

It was up to Bernie to finish the sentence. "Laura's dad, my father-in-law, was a firefighter too. That's how we met, actually. I was just young enough to have the stones to ask out the captain's daughter." For a split second a happy memory brightened Bernie's face before the sorrow returned. "Captain Davis died in the Towers on 9-11. We thought that our Cooper having his grandfather's same eyes was like a way for him to live on. It made Laura's mom so happy when she saw him for the first time."

Bernie lowered his head and sighed before turning his eyes upward toward the ceiling and the heavens beyond. "But I guess we've got two pairs of baby blues looking down on us now."

A single tear slowly made its way down the heartbroken father's face. "It helps me, though, to know that somebody was there waiting for Cooper when he got to Heaven. That he has somebody to watch out for him up there." Bernie briefly let go of his wife's hand to wipe another tear from his eyes. "I'm sorry. We'll leave you alone now. We just wanted you to know who our son was.

Wanted you to be able to think of Cooper when it gets late at night and you're tired and you need that extra motivation to keep going."

"Thank you," Isaac managed to reply despite the lump stuck in his throat. "I know how hard this must have been for you and we thank you, truly, for helping us get to know your baby boy."

THIRTY-SIX

Finally recovered from the gloom that settled over his office after the Simanki's visit earlier that day, Isaac once again found himself seated at a workstation in his lab well past the time when the rest of his colleagues had gone home. *It should not be this difficult*, Isaac thought. He felt like he still had a lot of work to make up after missing time for the White House meeting earlier in the week. Isaac rubbed his hands back and forth over his buzz cut hair and then down to massage the back of his shoulders. He had been staring at the same microscope for the past hour and a half and now had a killer crick in his neck.

"Come on, Dr. Carlson," Isaac told himself. "You do this sort of thing all the time. It's just a virus. Figure it out."

In theory, Isaac's pep talk was correct. 'All' he was doing was running tests to try to figure out what the virus was. Easy enough. "Except when it's not," he muttered in frustration.

The process had started with the arrival of the first patient files. Standard operating procedure at the various hospitals meant that Isaac and his team had access to the results of a number of tests, including complete blood counts, MRIs, and sonograms of the localized pain that many of the patients complained about. Of most use to the task force were the blood counts, since those told them if there were any drugs in the person's system or any so-called red-flags in the blood cell count.

"And these unfortunate souls," Isaac recalled, "all had CD4 cell levels below two hundred. Just like with AIDS. Except it's not AIDS. We tested for that. Even the guy with HIV hadn't crossed over yet." Isaac sighed heavily. "So it walks like AIDS, and it talks like AIDS, but it's not AIDS. It's *Super*AIDS," he declared, his voice rising in snarky indignation of the fact that, at the moment, this virus was kicking his ass.

The sound of an industrial-sized vacuum cleaner jarred Isaac, startling him as it took his sleep-deprived brain a minute to remember that the custodian usually cleaned his office right about this time of night.

"Hola, Marconi," Isaac said as the gray jumpsuit-clad office custodian turned off the vacuum for a moment and leaned against the door to Isaac's lab. Marconi knew enough to know not to touch anything in Dr. Carlson's lab, and Isaac appreciated the fact that the other man respected his space. That had been a problem with other janitors. "Como você está?"

Over the years, Isaac and the Brazilian immigrant had struck up a friendship of sorts, with each one slowly teaching the other his native language.

"I am well. Thank you," Marconi replied in an accent that was getting less and less noticeable every year. "You work late again, no?"

"Sim," Isaac answered. "Um caso muito difícil." That was how their conversations generally went. Isaac doing his best to speak Portuguese, and Marconi likewise with English.

"Okay. Good luck. I clean now," the custodian said with a smile as he turned away from the lab and clicked on the vacuum once again.

Why can't everyone be like Marconi? Isaac thought as he stood up and stretched his back and arms. *He's nice enough, but he's not nosy. Just does his job, lives his life, and leaves me to do and live mine.* "We don't all have to be best friends," he said aloud – this comment directed at the absent Dr. Dupree. Keri had tried so hard to be friends with Isaac when she first started working for him almost nine years ago. "I'll give credit where credit is due, though," he added. "You stuck with it way longer than most."

Isaac was simply a loner. He knew how to be social or cordial when he needed to be. Understood the value of group work to approach problems from multiple angles. Always tried extremely hard to have an excellent bedside manner with patients . . . was noted for that, actually. "I just prefer to be alone," he informed the empty room. "Nothing wrong with that."

"There is, however, something wrong with this," Isaac said as he turned his attention back to the patient information sprawled across his black marble lab table. "There's an answer in here somewhere. I just have to find it."

****

With her husband out of the country, Keri Dupree suddenly had a lot of extra time on her hands. Especially on the weekends. This particular Saturday morning, the day after the Simanski visit and after Scott left for Hong Kong, Keri had slept late and planned on watching some trashy television reruns before maybe going into the lab for a little while in the afternoon. Unlike Isaac, Keri did not have any research equipment in her house. And although she understood the value of rest and allowing one's brain to rejuvenate itself, Keri also felt bad taking an entire day off when there was a killer virus running rampant.

The ringing of the telephone broke Keri out of her thoughts. Reaching forward from the couch, the still pajama-clad woman grabbed the phone off of the coffee table.

"Hello?"

"Hey, Keri, it's me." Five weeks ago she wouldn't have recognized the voice, but now Keri instantly knew it was David. That was the nature of task forces like theirs. Complete strangers became almost like family in the blink of an eye, and then when the crisis ended the family would disintegrate. Keri hoped she would keep in touch with her new friends, though. Especially David and his wife Mary. They seemed nice.

"David. Hey. What's up?"

"What are you doing?" he asked, avoiding her question.

"Oh, nothing much. Watching a little TV. How about you?" The doctors weren't in a habit of calling each other just to chat, but Keri knew that David hadn't flown home this weekend because the results of a test he was running would come back this afternoon. *Poor guy is probably bored*, Keri thought. *Alone by himself in a hotel room.*

"Same. TV. Nothing productive," David answered. "I was actually wondering if you might want to meet up for coffee or lunch or something. To be honest, I don't really know what to do with myself since I'm not back home in Atlanta this weekend."

Keri laughed. "I know how you feel. With Scott gone the house just feels empty." She thought for a minute, and then suggested: "why don't we grab a late lunch at that little sandwich shop by the office? I was planning on going in for a few hours anyway this afternoon."

"Sounds great. One o'clock?"

"Perfect. See you then," Keri agreed and then hung up, taking the TV off of mute just as a big 'Real Housewives' catfight was about to begin.

THIRTY-SEVEN

Keri met David at precisely 1:00pm at Apollo's, a small Greek sandwich shop about five minutes away from the NIH campus. Immediately, she could see that this wasn't going to be just a friendly co-worker lunch. David clearly had something on his mind.

Keri waited until after they placed their orders at the counter, paid, and found a table before she broke the ice. "Okay, what is it? You look like you're itching to talk to me about something."

David laughed as he relaxed back into his chair. "Was I that obvious?"

His lunch partner smiled and nodded in response.

"It's nothing bad, if that's what you were thinking," explained David. "I just want your insight on something. Or, rather, someone."

Keri looked at him quizzically. "Who?"

"One beef gyro and one chicken?" interrupted a waiter carrying their sandwiches.

"Yeah, right here," David answered. After the teenaged employee walked away, David continued: "I want your insight on Isaac."

Keri held her index finger up in the air to ask for a minute while she finished chewing a bite of her sandwich. Finally she replied: "I don't know how much help I can be. What kind of insight are you talking about?"

"What makes him tick?" the CDC doctor responded immediately. "He's obviously a very complicated person, and I just feel like if I knew a little more about him then we would be able to work better together."

Now it was Keri's turn to lean back in her chair. "You're right," she sighed. "He is complicated. I've been working with him for eight years, almost nine, and I still don't understand a lot of what he says or does."

David nodded his head, acknowledging what Keri was saying. "I figured as much. But any kind of info would be useful. And, I know, we probably should have had this conversation a month ago."

Keri smiled and nodded. "Yeah, probably." Taking another bite of her sandwich, she said: "well, not to go all shrink on you, but I think Isaac's childhood had a lot to do with who he is now. He doesn't talk about it much, but apparently his parents were never really supportive of him beyond the financial. It seems like he was more of a shiny toy they could bring out and show off to friends but then ignore the rest of the time."

"That's awful," David commented.

"Yeah. So, like a lot of kids, he did everything he could to try to win their attention and approval. I think that's why he's such a perfectionist."

David nodded. "Maybe if I'm absolutely perfect, Mommy and Daddy will love me."

"Something like that," Keri replied.

"But what about his, oh what's the best way to put it –"

"Grouchiness?" Keri offered. "Impatience with others? Occasional jackass-ery?"

David laughed. "I was going to go with 'lack of social ability.'"

"That works too. Honestly, on that one," Keri answered, "I just think he never learned how. He's an only child, left to fend for himself a lot, and probably didn't have many friends in school. He admitted to me one time that he was always the nerdiest one in his class."

"Well so was I," replied David. "Although, maybe not. There's a big difference between smartest and nerdiest."

"A huge difference," Keri agreed. She suddenly felt a strong impulse to stand up for her boss. "Isaac's not a bad guy, I don't think. Yeah, he's rough around the edges and his attitude could use a lot of work. But he really cares about the cases he gets and the patients he treats. He won't rest until we find a solution for this virus. I guarantee you he's at the lab right now working."

David thought for a minute about everything that Keri had just told him. "So if he snaps at me for something, I should remember that it's probably just his frustration with the case spilling over."

"Exactly."

David nodded. "And when he turns down our offers for dinner or whatever, it's just because he doesn't really know how to have friends."

"True," answered Keri. "Sad, but true."

"Okay. That actually helps a lot," David said. Looking down at Keri's plate, he asked, "are you going to finish your sandwich or are you done?"

"Oh, I'm done. I can never eat a full sandwich here. They're too big."

"So you're ready to go?"

"Yep," she replied, standing up from the table. "That test for the virus won't create itself."

THIRTY-EIGHT

The fight against a deadly virus doesn't actually resemble much of a fight at all. There are very few, if any, action-packed scenes. No high-speed car chases. No shoot-outs. No impassioned speeches in front of large crowds. Instead, it's just a group of doctors logging hour after hour in research labs, trying one combination after another until they finally unlock the key to the mystery. It's monotonous, tiring, seemingly never-ending work, but it must be done. And as easy as it would have been for Isaac and his team to get discouraged and lose their edge, they knew that at the same time that they were in the lab working, there were people in hospitals dying. The task force members knew that because their leader wouldn't let them forget it.

Every morning, before the rest of the doctors arrived, Isaac looked through the stack of patient files and picked one out. Then he printed off a large color copy of that patient's picture and taped it and the person's name to the whiteboard in the middle of the main research lab. It was the patient of the day. A couple of times, when they didn't have any new files, Isaac put up a picture of a patient's child or mother or father instead. He called it their daily 'motivational.' And today's motivational was Chuck McKenna from Providence, Oklahoma.

****

Providence, Oklahoma is a small town. Not the kind of small town where everyone knows each other, but small enough where if you don't know a particular person, chances are you know someone who does. A two-degrees of separation kind of town. Two Super Wal-Marts and a hospital made Providence a regional hub for a section of the state that had far more cows per square mile than people.

The lone exception to the two-degrees of separation rule in Providence was the McKennas. Everyone knew the McKennas. Elijah McKenna had been one of the first to settle in the area – part of the "Boomer Sooner" land run in 1889 – and every generation thereafter had managed to leave its mark on the town. They were probably as close to a patrician family as it was possible to have in Oklahoma, with the first born son always taking over operation of the large family farm, and the daughters and second and third sons pursuing careers in other areas. There had been a veterinarian McKenna, a doctor McKenna, a preacher McKenna, a bank president, a mailman, and more than a few nurses and teachers.

The current McKenna clan was presided over by its patriarch, Big John. Big John's eldest boy, Little John, was actually a good six inches taller and seventy-five pounds heavier than his daddy. There was also Bobbie McKenna Jacobson, a third-grade teacher at Providence Elementary, and Chuck McKenna, the forty-three year old town sheriff. Chuck had enlisted in the Army straight out of high school, saw action in the first Gulf War, and had been the best sheriff anyone could remember for the past fifteen years.

Today, though, a newcomer to Providence wouldn't hear about Chuck's service in the military or his work to keep his jurisdiction safe from things like methamphetamines that had ravaged so many other rural areas. No, all any newcomers would know was that "Sheriff Chuck" needed their prayers. Everywhere anyone went in Providence, there were signs declaring support and prayers for Sheriff Chuck and his family. At the church. At the schools. At the bank. Even on a billboard by the interstate. The people in the town of Providence believed in the power of prayer, and Chuck McKenna needed all of the divine intervention that he could get.

An hour or so up the road in Norman, Chuck's wife Shannon sat in vigil beside her husband's hospital bed. Chuck had been accidentally shot on a hunting trip, and his initial prognosis had been for a full and complete recovery. Everyone in town had laughed about it; they even teased his buddy who shot him, calling him Dick Cheney.

But no one was laughing now. One week to the day after Chuck underwent surgery in Providence to remove buckshot from his arms and back, he started running a fever. Shannon got him to take some Tylenol and advised him to not push himself too hard that day, but Sheriff Chuck was determined to resume his duties. By the time he returned home that night to their cookie-cutter house in the only new(ish) subdivision in town, Chuck's fever was raging, his skin was pale and clammy, and he had begun coughing up blood. This was no post-surgery infection, and Shannon knew it.

Now, nine days later (sixteen days post-surgery), the sheriff's wife still hadn't fully come to terms with the seriousness of her husband's illness. He had been examined by several different doctors – a specialist had even come down from Oklahoma City – but Chuck wasn't getting any better. In fact, he kept getting worse.

A nurse slipped quietly into the room to check Sheriff McKenna's vital signs. The patient was asleep and she didn't want to wake him, even though he had been sleeping more and more lately and the veteran nurse got the feeling that pretty soon the brown haired, brown eyed man would fall asleep for the last time and not wake up again. The woman smiled gently at Mrs. McKenna and at the flowers, cards, and balloons filling the room. This man was clearly adored by many people. There was even a giant poster board hanging on the wall that had been signed by all of the members of the Providence High School football team, which for a place like Providence meant that it might as well have been signed by Justin Bieber. High school football players in their small town were miniature gods in teenaged bodies, and everyone who came to visit the sheriff remarked how special the signed poster was.

For Chuck, though, the most special gift in the room was the stuffed alligator lying at his feet. Chuck and Shannon were parents to three children, two boys and a girl, and the little girl had been a surprise. The boys were both in high school, but little Ainsley was still only five. Being a McKenna, the precocious toe-headed cutie decided that her daddy needed her favorite stuffed animal more than she did. Consequently, Stacy the Alligator now kept watch over her new owner at the foot of the hospital bed.

"Any improvement?" Shannon asked the nurse hopefully.

The other woman shook her head back and forth. "No ma'am. I'm sorry."

"That's alright," the patient's wife said with a brave smile. "He'll get better soon. He's a fighter."

All that the nurse could bring herself to say was "yes ma'am" as she exited the room. It was an uplifting yet vague reply, since she didn't want to upset Mrs. McKenna but she wasn't going to lie to her either.

Chuck's attending physician walked by just as his nurse closed the door to the room. "Excuse me, doctor?" she called out.

"Yes?"

"I was just wondering," the nurse began tentatively, "regarding this patient here, Mr. McKenna –"

"What about him?" the doctor asked.

"Well, sir, his wife still seems to think that he's going to get better. And I know I'm not the doctor, you are, but I've been around a long time and I've gotten pretty good at telling which patients will get to go home and which ones we'll be rolling down to the morgue."

The doctor sighed and pursed his lips together, shoving his hands down into the pockets of his white lab coat. In a hushed tone, he finally replied: "off the record, I think you're right. I think he's got a week left, maybe two. But," he added, "since I also have no idea what made him get sick so suddenly, I'm not willing to rule out the possibility that he'll recover just as quickly as he got sick."

The nurse nodded her head in understanding. "Do you think it could be that virus that the CDC put out a warning for?"

Normally the attending didn't like nurses who tried to play doctor, but this particular nurse had been at the hospital for almost as long as he had been alive, so he respected her work and her opinion.

"I don't know," the doctor answered. "Possibly. But even if it is, that doesn't help us any. The CDC doesn't have a treatment for it; they've just said the virus is out there." He shook his head. "No, unfortunately, all we can do for Mr. McKenna here is treat his symptoms, make him comfortable, and pray for a miracle."

THIRTY-NINE

By this point, after working together all day every day for five weeks, there were certain things that the task force knew they could expect. Leah would dress like a college sophomore studying for exams in the library, Isaac would at some point in the day be grumpy and snap at whoever was unlucky enough to be around him, and David would drop everything at 3:45pm to call his kids as soon as they got home from school. The six doctors had also come to recognize the soft three-rap knock that belonged to the receptionist, Lois. The middle-aged woman had a way of dropping in at least once or twice a week to say hello and see how things were going. The doctors couldn't decide if her visits to the third floor were a welcome break, annoying, or both.

On this particular Wednesday, Lois' knock found the task force members in the main research lab, each person working on a different potential test for the virus.

"Hi," Lois began, peeking her head around the door. "Sorry to interrupt."

Keri was closest to the exit and thus took it upon herself to be the one to answer. "No problem. What can I do for you?"

The other woman stepped farther into the room. "I actually came up here looking for Dr. Russo." Hearing his name, Anthony raised his head from a microscope. "Your wife is here, sir."

"Angela's here?" he asked, confused. Mrs. Russo hadn't visited him at work in years.

"Yep, she's downstairs. And actually," the receptionist continued, "she was hoping to come up here. She brought lunch for everyone."

At the mention of lunch, Gill's head shot up. "Did you say food?"

Lois laughed. "Well, technically, I said lunch."

"I think we could all use a break for some food," Anthony said. "Let's go downstairs, Lois. I'll help Angela carry up whatever it is that she brought."

****

Anthony and his stereotypically Italian wife returned a few minutes later carrying large shopping bags full of food. The couple placed the bags in the middle of the table in Conference Room D and began pulling out container after container of freshly-made, delicious-smelling Italian food.

"I wasn't sure what everyone would like, so I just brought a little bit of everything," Angela Russo said with a smile. "Various kinds of pastas and sauces so you can mix and match what you want. There's also bread and salad."

"Mrs. Russo, you are my hero," Gill said unabashedly. He enveloped the portly woman in a big bear hug, even as he reached over her shoulder to grab a bread roll from the table.

"Alright, that's enough, Gill," Anthony said in a good-natured yet protective voice. "Get your own wife."

"I am. Soon," the younger doctor responded with a grin, taking a bite out of the roll. "Three months from yesterday I'll be a married man."

"Oh that's wonderful," said Angela, linking her arm through her husband's. "Anthony and I have been married for forty-one years now. Marriage is such a blessing."

"Amen to that," David chimed in, then added: "thank you so much for bringing us all of this food. It looks amazing."

"Yes, thank you," Leah agreed. "Did you make it all yourself?" Having spent much more time with the Russos than the other doctors, Leah was aware that Mrs. Russo was a very accomplished cook.

Angela nodded her graying, brown head of hair up and down in reply. "Most of it. The bread, I must admit, is store bought. I was going to make that too but I ran out of time."

"My Angela is the best cook in Baltimore," Anthony said, beaming proudly as he grabbed a plate and loaded it high with pasta. "She's probably the best in all of Maryland. Try the ziti, you guys. Homemade. Just like they do it back in Italy."

"Oh, it's not that great," Angela said bashfully.

"Don't listen to her. It's amazing. She's amazing," the lunch chef's husband insisted.

There was a collective sigh in the room as the other five doctors watched Anthony and Angela interact. For David and Gill, the sigh was for the lives and women that they had to leave back home in Atlanta. For Keri, it was a wish that she and her husband could have a doting marriage like that. Leah sighed because she wanted someone, anyone, to look at her the way that Anthony was looking at Angela. And Isaac sighed in a rare moment of reflection on what his life could be like if he didn't have trust issues and he wasn't always alone.

****

The morning after the NIH task force's Italian feast, a man named Joseph sat at his kitchen counter, eating a bowl of cereal and listening to the news before he had to head in to work. They were talking about a virus, *his* virus, and the proud papa beamed from ear to ear as the reporter spoke:

"Some in the medical community have begun calling the mysterious illness SuperAIDS because of the similarity of symptoms. White House officials continue to insist that the American population is safe, but doctors at hospitals across the country are now starting to question that claim as twenty deaths are now linked to the sickness and another five people are currently hospitalized with similar symptoms."

Joseph nearly choked on his breakfast when he heard the latest infection totals. "Twenty dead?" he asked aloud. "And at least five more headed that direction?" Joseph shook his head. "You're certainly causing a lot more trouble than I expected," he said, looking down and talking through the floor to the secret lab that once housed his viral invention. "You didn't kill this many of the mice when we tested you. I guess I got the dosage wrong when I mixed up the human batches." For a split second, Joseph felt a twinge of what might have been mistaken for regret. Not regret over the people dying. Certainly not. Rather, it was regret that something hadn't gone exactly as he planned or expected.

The moment quickly passed, though, and Joseph chuckled to himself as he put his bowl in the sink and grabbed his car keys off the counter. "I really have created a monster, haven't I?"

FORTY

"Who do you think it is today?" Leah asked Gill as they rode the elevator together up to their third floor offices and labs. It wasn't unusual for members of the task force to arrive at the same time in the mornings – they all kept basically the same schedule. Except for Isaac, of course, who ninety-nine times out of one hundred arrived earlier and stayed later than anyone else. The man was a machine.

"What do you mean?" Gill replied. "Our motivational patient of the day?"

"Yeah," answered Leah, nodding. The painfully shy young woman had come out of her shell a lot during her time working on the task force, and her colleagues all agreed that she was a very nice, amiable person.

"I don't know," said Gill in reference to who the patient of the day would be. Stepping off the elevator, he lowered his voice as he added: "I get why Isaac does it, to keep us motivated and all, but it's still kinda creepy to have that big picture of a dead person staring at you all day long."

Leah's short legs struggled to keep up with Gill's long strides as the two doctors made their way down the hall to their lab. "I don't know," she said pensively. "I kind of like it. It reminds me what we're working for."

Dr. Pingrey looked at his counterpart skeptically. "Yeah, but if we keep putting up pictures and talking about them then we're going to start having the ghosts of patients past following us around everywhere."

Leah busted out laughing at Gill's final comment. "The ghosts of patients past?" She laughed some more. "Come on, dude."

"I'm serious," Gill replied, and Leah could see that he was. "Just ask Anthony over there; he'll agree with me."

"Agree with you about what?" asked the older doctor who had arrived at work a few minutes earlier.

Leah smirked. "Gill thinks that by putting up pictures of the patients then we're inviting their ghosts to haunt us."

Much to Dr. Mann's chagrin, the devoutly Catholic Anthony nodded his head in agreement. "Sure, it's possible, if their souls are in Purgatory." He then smiled gently at his young assistant. "Don't look so surprised, Leah. I've talked to you about Church teachings before."

Isaac, who had been sitting unnoticed at a corner table until now, cleared his throat loudly. "I think that's enough religious talk today. Ghosts or no ghosts, God or no God, we still have a virus to fight."

The other doctors grumbled in reply but dispersed nonetheless to their workstations. Anthony, though, wanted to make sure he got in one good, clean shot at the task force leader.

"You know, Carlson, I know it makes you uncomfortable when people refer to God as being someone other than you, but every once in a while religion is going to come up as a topic of conversation. This is a talkative group, for better or worse. And if we talk about sports, and fashion, and family, and movies, and seemingly everything else under the sun, then occasionally you're going to hear the word God."

"Are you finished?" Isaac coolly replied.

"Yep," Anthony answered, feeling quite good about himself and his little speech.

"Good. Then maybe you and God can chat with the ghost of today's motivational and ask her how the fuck we're supposed to make this test to screen for the virus that killed her."

Everyone in the room cringed. Isaac was mad. Madder than they had ever seen him. However, thanks to their lunchtime conversation a couple of days before, both Keri and David knew that Isaac wasn't actually mad at them. He was mad at the virus. And mad at himself for not figuring out the answer yet.

****

That day's motivational patient, the one with whom Anthony was supposed to consult, was a fifty-year-old Boston woman named Diane Parker. Born and raised in Charlestown, Diane had worked her way through school at Boston University and slowly risen up the ranks of an educational supply company until she was one of its senior managers. She was divorced with two grown children who she didn't see or talk to very often, an ex-husband who she hated, and a smoking habit that was killing her. Or, to be more accurate, a smoking habit that had been killing her. Because now what was killing Diane Parker was the same thing that had killed Chuck McKenna and Marcus Johnson and Elena Hernandez, and Taylor Stone and Edna Jenkins and many others between them.

Doctors at Massachusetts General Hospital couldn't figure it out. Medical students from Harvard, Tufts, BU, and the myriad other universities in Boston studied her case – a few lucky post-graduate students even got to visit and observe the mystery patient – but still no one could explain how an otherwise healthy middle-aged woman went from battling a very beatable case of lung cancer to knocking on death's door in a matter of weeks.

Diane's two children and their spouses had come to see her, even though they really didn't know what to do or say. She had never been particularly close to them . . . that was their father's department. So much so that he received full custody of both girls after the divorce. That had been nearly ten years ago, and Diane and her children had only grown farther apart since then.

It was sad, really, this woman who was so clearly dying yet also so painfully alone. The nurses in the infectious diseases unit took pity on her and sat by Diane's bedside when they had any spare time, talking to her or reading books aloud. At this point, though, Diane couldn't hear the nurses anymore. Her version of the supervirus had hit hard with a fever, followed by diarrhea, followed by skin lesions so disgusting that doctors had to sedate Ms. Parker to prevent her from going into shock at the sight of them. The fever had now persisted for so long that she was in a coma with brain damage.

Yes, Diane Parker was dying, and aside from a few hospital nurses, the people who cared the most were six doctors she had never met, working for an agency she had never heard of, to defeat a virus that she never saw coming.

FORTY-ONE

"Excuse me, Dr. Malhotra?"

Lois the receptionist stuck her head through the cracked conference room doorway once again. "You have a phone call."

By unanimous agreement of the task force members, all cell phones, pagers, and any other type of communication device were turned off during their designated group meetings. The team didn't want anything distracting them while they worked. The only electronic anything in the room was a smartphone that Isaac had configured to send him updates on patients. Everything else could wait. Except right now, it seemed.

"Take a message," David said. He liked the receptionist; she was friendly and good at her job and had gone out of her way to make him feel welcome at NIH. Lois and her husband had even hosted him for dinner one night at their home. The woman's one flaw, though, was her timing. She always seemed to interrupt during something important.

"I'm sorry, sir," Lois continued, "but it's your wife. She says it's an emergency."

David let loose a grumbled, exacerbated sigh and rolled his eyes as he stood up. "I'm sorry, y'all. I'll be right back."

After the other man had followed Lois back out of the room, Isaac declared, "and *that* is another reason to never get married."

Keri knew her boss was a loner; a workaholic who was married to his job. But she also knew that, at least on this topic, he was wrong. "If any woman ever agreed to marry you I would personally examine her for brain damage."

A chorus of shocked and muffled laughs filled the room as the rest of the doctors couldn't believe Keri had the gumption to call out Isaac like that. Even though they had all been thinking some version of the same thing.

Isaac didn't respond. Instead, he just gave Keri his patented disapproving stare before turning his attention to the files in front of him. Keri, however, had been working side-by-side with Isaac for far too long not to notice the brief glimpse of hurt that crossed his features when the other people in the room were laughing at his expense. *Poor guy,* Keri thought. *He can't help it. He's just not a social person. He doesn't know how.*

Sensing the pain that her renowned boss would never reveal, Dr. Dupree quickly came to his defense. "I'm just kidding, Isaac. It would definitely take a special woman to marry you, but she'd be a lucky special woman."

"Ha," Isaac answered. "Now who needs the head exam?"

The rest of the room laughed again, appreciative of the lighter tone and brief respite from studying charts of dead people. And Keri saw the slightest loosening of the tension in Isaac's shoulders – imperceptible to the others but a welcome sign for her. Dr. Isaac Carlson was tough, irritating, demanding, and uncompromising to a fault. But deep, deep down in his core, in the part of himself that he kept locked away from the rest of the world, was a mushy teddy bear of a man who was still in many regards trying to make people like him. So Keri pushed him, yes. And she teased him and she let him know when he was being a jerk. But she didn't push him too far. Isaac was, for her, the older brother she loved to hate – until someone outside of the family tried to say something against him. At which point she immediately sprang to his defense.

Isaac knew it, too. He knew that Keri Dupree knew him better than anyone else ever had, which was one of the main reasons why he kept sabotaging any attempts by other labs to steal her away. Sensing he was being watched, Isaac quickly cut his eyes over in the direction of his deputy.

"Quit staring," he muttered where only Keri could hear him. "Get back to work."

****

"What is it, Mary?" David asked as soon as he picked up the phone in an office down the hall from the conference room. "I'm in the middle of a meeting."

David regretted his tone as soon as his wife began to speak. Histrionics filled the air as the normally composed housewife yelled into the receiver: "I don't care that you're in a meeting! You have to come home. Now!"

Mary Malhotra, née Lewiston, was not one to become unduly emotional. It had caused quite a stir when the blonde, Southern debutant had announced her intention to marry the son of Indian immigrants, and while Mary wasn't nearly as snooty or WASP-ish as her parents, she still usually retained an air of composure about her that only generations of breeding and culture could achieve.

All of which combined to make David all the more worried by his wife's opening statement. "What is it? What happened?"

"The twins were in a wreck," Mary managed to choke out through her tears. "Sharon from down the street was picking up all of the kids from school – it was her day for carpool – and since Matty and Jane were the last ones to get to the car they both jumped in the back of the station wagon. In that little seat that faces backwards?"

"Yeah," David said in response, knowing his wife wouldn't continue until he acknowledged that he knew what seat she was talking about. *As if that matters right now*, he thought.

"They were rear-ended. Jane and Matty are both in surgery," Mary exclaimed, her histrionics returning in full force. "David you have to come home. You and I both know that there are flights every hour on the hour from

Reagan to Hartsfield," she added, referencing the airports in Washington, DC and Atlanta. "Come home."

The father and the doctor in David combined to spring him into action. "I'm coming" was all he said before he dropped the phone back on the desk and took off at a full sprint in the direction of the task force's conference room. Reaching the room where his colleagues were still working, David burst open the door and went immediately to his seat, grabbing his suit jacket off the back of his chair and his briefcase from the floor.

"What in the world?" Isaac asked.

"I've gotta go," an out-of-breath David answered as he turned to leave. "My kids were in an accident. I've gotta go."

And without another word he was gone, leaving a room full of confused doctors in his wake.

****

The disturbing thought hit David as he sped along the interstate on his way to Ronald Reagan National Airport. Once again he found himself rushing to get to a hospital where someone he knew might have to get a blood transfusion, and that blood could be carrying a virus that would kill them. *Shit*, he thought as he quickly grabbed his cell phone and hit speed dial for his wife. "Please picked up," David prayed aloud. "Please pick up."

Just as he was expecting the call to flip over to Mary's voicemail, she answered. "Are you on your way?" David's wife asked. A little bit of the usual calm had returned to her voice – something David took to be a good sign.

"Listen, honey, I need you to get their doctor on the phone. I need to talk to him."

"Well, it's a her," Mary corrected, "but I can't. Both of the twins are in surgery. But they said they should be fi–"

"No!" David yelled, interrupting his wife before she could finish her sentence with the word 'fine.' "No!" he repeated. "Pull the doctors out of surgery. I don't care. I have to talk to them!"

The calm in Mary's voice as she told him she couldn't do that hit Dr. Malhotra like a ton of bricks, with the realization settling in that it was already too late. If his children needed blood transfusions, they had probably already received them. And if that blood was tainted, there was nothing he could do.

Strangely enough, as David pulled into the long-term parking lot at the airport, he was able to find a small amount of solace in something that had until that point infuriated him: the virus' quick rate of progression. There would be no waiting around for months or years to see if any symptoms appeared. If Matthew or Jane had the illness, they would know within the next week. It was a very small amount of solace, indeed.

FORTY-TWO

A soft knock on the door of his son's hospital room woke David from the first sleep he had gotten in days. He glanced quickly at the machines monitoring the boy's vital signs and then patted the sleeping Matthew's arm before standing up and walking over to the door and the doctor waiting just outside the room.

Gently closing the door behind him, David asked: "what is it?"

Even though the attending physician standing in front of him was almost his same age, height, and build, David got the impression that the other man was nervous. And he was correct. David Malhotra was a legend in his Atlanta medical community, and the doctor standing before him felt like he was meeting one of The Beatles.

"I'm so, so sorry to bother you . . . especially at a time like this," the other man began.

David, tired and hungry and worried and wanting to be back in the room with his son, simply repeated: "what is it?"

"I know you're on the task force dealing with the mysterious virus that some people are calling SuperAIDS."

"Yes?" David prodded, still irritated to be taken away from his son. His wife was next door in their daughter's room, and the two parents kept switching back and forth so neither of the twins would ever be left alone. *Except right now*, he thought.

"I'm the chief immunologist here at Children's," the doctor explained, referring to the well-regarded children's hospital with branches around the Atlanta area. Dr. Malhotra's kids had been taken to the Egleston campus, which was the closest to where their car wreck occurred and was also next door to David's office at the CDC. "I have a patient here who is exhibiting all of the symptoms of your virus."

David sighed, yawned, and rubbed his fingers back and forth over his tired eyes. "I'm really sorry to hear that," he finally answered, "and part of me would really like to go with you to examine the kid. But that's my son in there," David said, gesturing behind him. "And my daughter is right next door. They were in a car accident and just got out of surgery. I can't leave them right now."

The other doctor grimaced and nodded his head. "I've got three kids of my own. I understand. But," he added, "if you do decide you want to come see the boy, we're in the South Wing. Fifth floor. Just ask for me, Dr. Jefferson."

"Alright," David replied. "Now if you'll excuse me . . ." he added, then turned and reentered young Matty's room without finishing his sentence.

****

Mary Malhotra watched through the window as her husband continued his vigil by their daughter's bedside. Earlier it had been their son – whichever child David was with at that moment, he was watching him or her like a hawk. Mary noticed that one of the nurses had come to stand beside her. "It's almost like he's looking for something," Mary said to no one in particular.

The nurse gently patted Matthew and Jane's mom on her shoulder. "Everyone reacts to trauma differently. He'll be fine."

"But he's a doctor," Mary protested.

The other woman nodded knowingly. "He's a research doctor – what he does in his lab is completely different from what we do here. Plus," she added, "it's always harder when it's your own kid. Or kids."

Mrs. Malhotra sighed. "I suppose you're right. I just wish I could convince David to go home at least for a little bit. Take a shower; change his clothes. He's starting to smell."

Both women laughed at that last remark. The nurse then patted Mary's shoulder again and said comfortingly: "he'll be fine, ma'am. You'll see."

FORTY-THREE

"Dr. Malhotra, you came!" exclaimed a relieved Dr. Jefferson has he emerged from behind a large nurses' station desk and shook David's hand. Dr. Jefferson was no rookie and was well-regarded in the hospital, but he was also the first to admit that the virus his patient was fighting was way out of his league.

"My wife told me to," David replied honestly. Mary Malhotra had quite literally ordered her husband to take a break from his bedside vigil before he drove himself crazy. 'All you do all day long is sit there and stare at them. They're going to be fine. The doctors said so. Get out of here for a while.'

"Well, you'll have to tell her I said thank you," quipped a visibly relieved Phil Jefferson. "I know you probably don't want to waste any time, so let me take you to see the patient."

"What was he originally here for?" David asked as they walked down the hall toward the isolation rooms.

Dr. Jefferson turned sideways to look at David in surprise. "How did you know he wasn't here for this illness?"

Realizing his mistake, David simply shrugged his shoulders. "Lucky guess." *Pull it together, David*, he told himself. *We don't want people to know about the link to the blood transfusing, because then they'd start refusing them and die because of that*. He and Isaac had told Daniel Bader's wife, but that was a special case. David's twins were also special cases, but that was why he was keeping his 'bedside vigil' as Mary called it. He wanted to know the second either of his children started exhibiting any symptoms of the virus.

Luckily, the doctor beside him didn't seem to think that David's answer was suspicious. "Well, your lucky guess was right on the money. The patient's name is Julius Wilkes," Dr. Jefferson said as he came to a stop outside the boy's room. "He's fifteen-years-old and from a really rough area of Downtown. Julius originally came to us with a gunshot wound."

"Gang violence?" David asked.

"Possibly, but not in the way you're thinking. He was asleep in his bedroom when a stray bullet came through the window."

David grimaced. "That's awful. Poor kid."

"We had to operate to remove the bullet from his back," Phil Jefferson continued, "and he stayed three days after that. Another five days later, Julius was back and complaining of a sore throat, a headache, joint pain, and severe diarrhea."

"Let me guess, he thought the symptoms were side effects from the surgery."

"Correct again," the Children's doctor answered. "Is that common with these patients?"

"Somewhat," David said. "How long's he been here now?"

"Fourteen days."

David lowered his voice in case any family members or gossipy nurses were listening. "He's got another week. Two at the very most. He's young and otherwise healthy, which helps. But we haven't had any last longer than a month."

"Don't you want to examine him or anything?"

David shook his head no. "I don't need to. The symptoms you listed are consistent, and I can see the skin lesions from here. He's got the virus."

A pained expression covered Dr. Jefferson's face as he received the news. "How many cases have y'all had now?"

"Counting this kid? Twenty-four." David sighed. "I'm sorry I don't have better news for you. And I should probably be getting back."

"Right, of course."

David shook the other doctor's hand and started walking back down the hallway. After a few steps, he stopped and turned. "Dr. Jefferson?" he called out.

"Yes?"

"You should go ahead and tell his family. Give them time to prepare."

****

The gated community in Northeast Atlanta where the Malhotra family lived had always been a peaceful place for David. Driving home from a stressful day at work, he would smile at older couples out walking together or kids riding their bikes. When David really thought about it, he realized that he liked where he lived so much because it was like the American Dream had been put into neighborhood form. Although mostly white and Protestant, there was a good amount of racial and ethnic diversity, a wide range of religious beliefs, and street after street of people who worked hard and rose through the socioeconomic ladder just like David had. His neighbors were all well-off like he was, but it certainly wasn't like other old money areas of the city. No, this neighborhood's motto might as well have been 'work hard, live right, and you will be rewarded.'

None of those relaxed, happy thoughts hit David today, though, as he made his way through the tree lined streets to his house. Mary had literally commanded him to come home and at the very least shower, shave, and change clothes. "It wouldn't hurt you to get a good night's sleep either," she had said. "Plus I know the dogs will go crazy when they see you."

The thought of his family's two big dogs was enough to bring a smile to David's face as he pulled into the garage. He hadn't realized how much he missed them while being up in Maryland, but now he was really excited to see the pets again.

And they were happy to see him. David couldn't help but laugh when, as soon as he went inside the house, a combined one hundred fifty pounds of canine literally tackled him to the floor and started licking all over his face.

"Okay, okay, I know. I missed y'all too," David said as he laughed. "But come on, let me up. Gus, Isis – let me up." Gus the eighty-pound chocolate lab and Isis the seventy-pound golden retriever finally complied. Their owner wiped slobber off his face and fur off of his clothes as the family's cat, Macy, observed everything from her perch on top of the refrigerator. "If I didn't know any better, I would swear that your mom called and pull y'all up to that." The Malhotras were those kind of people . . . Gus, Isis, and Macy were members of the family. Four-legged children, if you will.

"And now," David said as he pushed his way past the still extremely excited dogs, "I need to go shower. Mom was right . . . I am starting to smell."

FORTY-FOUR

David's twins were released from the hospital a few days later. The families living on either side of the Malhotras and the retired couple from across the street had decorated the Malhotra mailbox with balloons and put up a big banner above their garage that read: 'Welcome Home Jane and Matty.' The woman across the street, Teena, had a key to the house because she had been taking care of the animals, and she decided that the inside of the home needed streamers and balloons as well. There was also a cake safely tucked away in the refrigerator to keep it out of reach of the dogs and cat.

A chorus of "welcome home" greeted the two young accident victims as their parents wheeled them up the sidewalk to the front door. Both Mary and David's parents had come over the day before to convert the downstairs living room and study into bedrooms where the kids could sleep until they were strong enough to consistently climb the stairs. Matty and Jane were both very lucky to have escaped the accident without any serious permanent damage, and their parents knew it. Jane broke a couple of ribs and had a compound fracture in her lower leg that required surgery to fix. Matthew had broken his ankle and separated his shoulder – the shoulder needing an operation. They both also had a small amount of internal bleeding, but the surgeons got that under control quickly. *Aside from that, just cuts and bruises*, David thought as he stood back and watched his kids talking and laughing with their grandparents and neighbors. *It could have been a lot worse.* Suddenly, the pleasant expression on David's face was replaced by one of uncertainty and fear. *It could still be a lot worse*, he reminded himself. *We're not in the clear yet.*

Mary Malhotra noticed the change in her husband's expression. He had been happy like everyone else, but now he was brooding in the corner with the same searching look that he had on his face for the past several days. *I've had about enough of that*, she decided before marching over to confront David.

"What is your problem?" Mary whispered accusingly. "This is a happy moment. Our kids are home from the hospital; they're going to be fine. Stop looking so . . . grumpy," she declared for lack of a better word.

David hadn't told his wife about the possibility of infection – he didn't want to worry her unless and until there was officially something to worry about. The expression that Mary mistook for grumpy was actually the face he used to concentrate while working. She just never saw him at his office so she didn't know that. But, as far as David was concerned, he was at work. He wasn't at a welcome home party for his kids. He was in a room with two potential virus patients, and it was his job as a member of the task force to watch them like a hawk for any signs or symptoms.

****

It started with a cough. The dining room that had been converted into Matty's sleeping quarters was directly below the master bedroom, and David heard the hacking cough almost as soon as it began.

"Where are you going?" a sleepy Mary asked when David got up out of bed.

"Matty is coughing. I'm going to bring him some water. It's fine. Go back to sleep."

Maybe it's just a cough, David thought as he hurried down the front stairs. "Oh please God, let it just be a cough."

It wasn't just a cough. Young Matthew's fever had already topped 103 degrees by the time David got to him and checked it, and the boy was both sweating profusely and shivering at the same time.

"Shit," David declared. "Shit!" he said again, this time his voice full of emotion as tears filled his eyes. Dr. Malhotra had read too many case files and seen too many patient photos to not recognize what was in front of him. Eight days post-surgery; post- *blood transfusion-involved* surgery. Cough. Fever. Night sweats. "Shit." It was the only word that David could think to say.

Even though he knew it wouldn't change the end result, the panicked father rushed back upstairs and told Mary that he was taking Matty to the hospital. She would have to stay at the house with Jane until either set of their parents could arrive to watch her.

"I'm not staying here! I'm going with you. We'll bring Jane too," Mary cried out as she struggled to change out of her pajama bottoms into jeans.

David calmly rested his hands on his wife's shoulders. "Look at me." When she didn't comply, he repeated: "Mary, honey, look at me."

Two very frightened blue eyes blinked upward at David. "It's the middle of the night. There won't be traffic. My parents can get here in half an hour. Forty-five minutes tops. Matty will be fine until you get to the hospital. Trust me."

Mrs. Malhotra closed her eyes and nodded her head in acquiescence. "Alright. But you call me as soon as you know anything."

"I will," David replied. He then kissed his wife on the forehead and hurried back downstairs to take his son to the hospital. As he pulled out of the driveway, the tears returned in droves as David realized that the boy in the backseat would never come home again.

****

"He has your virus, doesn't he?"

David heard the pain, the fear, and the anger in his wife's voice. "It's not my virus," he replied defensively. President Hughes had also called it David's virus, and the doctor didn't like the association then just as he didn't like it now.

Mary's tear-filled eyes looked up from their son's hospital bed to glare at her husband. "You knew," she said accusingly. "That's why you called wanting to talk to their doctors while they were in surgery. Why you watched them like a hawk while they were in recovery. You knew they might get it. And that's why you said he would be fine until I got to the hospital. Because you knew how long it would take him to . . ." Mary paused and struggled to swallow the large lump in her throat. "How long it would take him to die. You *knew*."

"But you're right," Mary added bitterly. "It's not your virus. It's his," she concluded, nodding her head in Matty's direction. The distraught mother closed her eyes to try to hold back her tears.

"Mary –" David said, reaching out to touch her arm.

She shrugged him away.

"Honey –" he tried again.

"Leave me alone, David. Leave us alone."

FORTY-FIVE

Funerals are terrible. They're sad, the weather hardly ever seems to cooperate, and there is always at least one awkward family member who says something inappropriate. Yes, funerals are terrible. But a funeral for a child? There are no words to describe a funeral for a child. As perhaps there shouldn't be . . . there should be no words for an event which, in a seemingly more just world, would never happen.

The memorial service for young Matthew David Malhotra was no exception. Well over half of their neighborhood was in attendance, as well as many children from Matty's school. The members of his soccer team also came – all of them wearing their jerseys. That was a particularly touching detail for the Malhotras, since Matty was being buried in his uniform. Dr. Malhotra's five fellow task force members did not make the trip down to Atlanta for the funeral, but only because David told them not to. He didn't want them to take time travelling that would otherwise be spent working on bringing the virus' deadly run to an end.

David's son had lived for another two and a half weeks at the hospital, but in the last week he was hardly ever conscious. As hard as it was, the certainty of the ending gave people a chance to say goodbye to the twelve-year-old. But even with the advance notice, the boy's death still shook everyone in their close-knit suburban community. Things like this weren't supposed to happen to people like them. It didn't seem fair.

The greatest example that life was unfair was found sitting in a wheelchair on the end of the first row at Grace Memorial Church. Jane Malhotra had been in the same accident. She had surgery on the same day, in the same hospital. They were twins, for Heaven's sake. But now Jane was alive and her brother Matty wasn't. And, because of that, the little girl on the front row felt very, very guilty. Thoughts of *it could've been me, it should've been me*, and *why wasn't it me?* kept running through her head.

Jane's distraught father knew the answer to the last question. It came down to blood type. Jane was B-positive; Matty was AB-negative. Their transfused blood came from different sources. Matty's was tainted; Jane's was clean.

David had tried to explain that fact to Mary several times while their son was still alive and then again in the four days since his passing. But Mrs. Malhotra didn't want to hear it. She didn't want anything to do with David right now. In her mind, this was his fault. He gave Matty the virus. Deep down, Mary probably knew that that wasn't true, but a mother's grief can cause people to say and do all sorts of things.

Mary wasn't alone in blaming David for Matty's death. He blamed himself, but for different reasons. The thought that wouldn't leave David was that he should've solved the puzzle sooner. If only he and the rest of the task force had already come up with a test to screen blood for the virus, his son could still be alive today.

The painful thoughts of the deceased's immediate family members were unknown to the hundreds of other people who packed into the non-denominational Protestant church for young Matthew's memorial service. All that the other attendants saw was grief, and there was plenty of that to go around as well. As first the pastor, then Matty's soccer coach, a favorite teacher, and finally Mary's brother Josh spoke from the lectern behind where the boy's body lay, all David could think was that he needed to leave. People respond to tragedy and grief in very personal, unique ways, and the esteemed medical researcher's response was an overwhelming urge to return to his lab at the CDC. David couldn't stand this anymore. He couldn't let any more families go through what his was going through right now.

David knew that Mary wouldn't understand – in fact, she would probably get even madder at him than she already was. *She'll understand one day*, David thought to himself. *She's too good of a person to want anyone else to have to die.*

The doctor wiped his eyes with the back of his hand as his brother-in-law finished the final eulogy of the service. Taking a deep breath, David stood up and offered his arm to his grief-stricken wife who, still angry with him, only accepted it because she didn't have the strength to stand up on her own.

PART III: COMING TO AN END

FORTY-SIX

Several days after his funeral, Matty Malhotra's picture remained up on the whiteboard at the National Institutes of Health. The team had decided that he would be their motivational patient of the day, every day, until the end. And now, that end was finally in sight. Isaac Carlson had never been this happy before in his entire life. Not medical school graduation, or his first million-dollar pharmaceutical deal, or being named to the Presidential Commission for the Study of Bioethical Issues could match this.

"I did it!" Isaac yelled at the top of his lungs as he literally ran out of his lab and began high-fiving everyone in sight. "I did it I did it I did it!" he continued to exclaim.

Keri emerged from the task force's conference room and stared, dumbfounded, at Isaac. *He clearly must be high or possessed or something, because Isaac Carlson is never that happy.*

"You did what?" she asked.

Isaac responded by taking his top deputy in his arms and swinging her around in a circle. "A test!" he said, beaming. "I did it! Or, rather, we did it," he quickly corrected. "But I've got it. A test for the virus. I've got it!"

In very short order, the number of doctors yelling with joy and running through the halls of the NIH jumped from one to five as Keri, Leah, Gill, and Anthony joined Isaac in his celebration. All of their late hours and tireless efforts had finally paid off: they had a way to test blood to make sure it didn't carry the deadly virus. In many ways it was these doctors' equivalent of Jonas Salk creating the polio vaccine, because now they had a way to stop patients from contracting the virus. They had finally won.

****

"So what do we think it was?" Keri asked as she took another giant sip from the bottle of champagne in her hand. She was reclined almost completely on the couch in Isaac's office with her face to the ceiling and her stocking-clad feet dangling off the end of the furniture.

"Who cares," Gill replied from the corner where he and a six-pack of beer had parked themselves almost an hour ago. After the giddy celebration of finally having a test for the virus came to an end and they had sent the screening formula out to hospitals near and far, the five task force members who remained in Maryland had bought out a local liquor store and come back to Isaac's office to bask further in their glory.

"The kid, for once, is correct," a very drunk Dr. Russo declared. "Who cares? We beat it. That's what matters."

The usually extremely composed Isaac leaned forward from behind his desk and hugged the now half-empty bottle of scotch in front of him. "No no no . . . Keri's got a point. She's a smart one, that Keri."

Everyone in the room giggled as Isaac slurred his words. They all liked him a lot better when he was drunk.

Isaac opened his mouth to speak again and then froze and looked around the room confusedly. "What were we talking about?"

"The virus," Leah answered. She wasn't much of a drinker and had consequently only consumed one beer – well, one beer plus the shot of tequila that Gill made everyone do together. Nevertheless, Dr. Mann was far and away the most sober person in the room. "Keri wants to know what caused the virus," she reminded the task force leader.

"Right. Right," Isaac repeated, still hugging his alcohol. "What caused it. I vote for . . ."

"Aliens!" Gill offered up from the corner, causing everyone to double over in laughter.

"Aliens?" asked Keri. "Come on. That's so 1990s. No . . . it was vampires. Everything is vampires nowadays."

"No way," Anthony broke in, gesturing in the air with his own bottle of wine. "Vampires would've drank the blood, not poisoned it." His fellow medical professionals nodded their heads in agreement and marveled at the oldest member of the group's keen insight.

"A mutation," Leah proposed after she sensed that the conspiracy theorists were finished with their fun. "A weird, brief, genetic mutation."

"By George, I think she's got it!" Isaac declared boisterously. Leah rolled her eyes as that last line issued in a whole new round of *My Fair Lady*-themed singing and dancing for the very happy, very drunk doctors.

FORTY-SEVEN

"Well look at you!" Isaac called out with a grin as he walked across the Roosevelt Room of the White House. He was talking to Daniel Bader – still officially the Chief of Staff and now slowly beginning to increase his work hours again.

"I know . . . not dead yet," Daniel joked as he gave Isaac his trademarked bone-crushing handshake. Three months after the triple bypass that had saved his life, Daniel Bader felt like a brand new man. "Unless that virus of yours has an extended dormant period that we don't know about."

"Oh God, I hope not," Isaac responded with a shudder. "I'd have to give my award back."

Daniel laughed. "I don't think we've ever had to strip anyone of their National Medal of Science before. This isn't cycling."

This time it was Dr. Carlson's turn to laugh. "No, no doping scandal here."

"You boys seem to be enjoying yourselves," Keri remarked as she joined them in the corner of the room. In recognition of their hard work and success, the entire task force had been invited to the White House to meet with President Hughes. Everyone except David was there. Dr. Malhotra had already returned to work at the CDC, but he refused to take part in any ceremonies or other events honoring the doctors' hard-won victory against the mysterious virus. Because, in David's mind, the task force failed. *He* failed. And he didn't want to have anything to do with any of it anymore.

"Hey, I'm alive. What's there not to enjoy?" Daniel asked in response to Keri's comment. "Although my wife is still pretty pissed at you, Carlson."

The middle-aged pathologist sighed. "I know. She'll probably hate me forever, but I was just trying to give her a heads up of what to watch for."

"What are you talking about?" asked Keri.

Daniel was the first one to respond. "Isaac was here at the White House when I had my heart attack. He and the other doctor, David, – poor man – came to the hospital in the motorcade. Although I still don't understand why," the Chief of Staff commented. "But anyway, they're all there at the hospital and the doctor says that I need a triple bypass. This genius here," he said, pointing to Isaac, "decides it's a good idea to tell my wife that the blood transfusion I'll get during the surgery might be carrying a deadly virus, and all she can do about it is wait a week to see if symptoms X, Y, or Z start showing up."

Keri rolled her eyes and shook her head in disbelief. "Nice one, Isaac."

Her boss was spared any more reminders of Mrs. Bader's wrath when the doors to the Roosevelt Room swung open and President Richard Hughes walked in. "Geniuses of the lab!" he declared with a smile. "Where's the champagne? I feel like celebrating."

FORTY-EIGHT

Isaac's palms were sweaty. So was his forehead. And his back. And his feet. *And other areas I don't care to mention*, the esteemed pathologist thought to himself as he fidgeted in his chair.

"I'm sorry, sir, but can you please try to sit still?" It was the third time that the beleaguered makeup artist had asked him to stop moving, and the young woman was clearly getting frustrated.

"I'm sorry. I'm sorry," Isaac repeated. "Just a little nervous, I guess."

"Oh. my. gosh," Keri declared, clutching at her chest in mock surprise. "The Dr. Isaac Carlson is nervous? No way!" It was rare for Keri to have such an easy opportunity to poke fun at Isaac, and she was enjoying making the most of it.

"Yeah yeah yeah," Isaac replied. "Have your fun." He made a decent effort to look wounded by Keri's teasing, but the truth was that he liked it. He had been made fun of many times in his life, but that had always been by mean-spirited school bullies or classmates. This teasing, though, was friendly. Good-natured. Directed towards a member of the in-crowd instead of the kid who had always been a loner. Sure, the virus outbreak and his leadership of the task force had won him numerous awards and been a boon to his pathology business, but more than anything else what Isaac gained the most from the past four months was friends. Or at least the closest thing to friends that he'd ever had.

"Okay, that about does it. You're all set, Dr. Carlson," the makeup artist said, visibly relieved to be finished with her difficult client.

"If you say so," responded Isaac as he rose from his chair and removed the white tissues that had been sticking out of his collar to keep makeup from staining his shirt. "I'll see you out there," he added, referencing Dr. Dupree, who would be joining him for an exclusive interview on America's top-rated daytime talk show. Now that the virus scare appeared to be over – the test Isaac created was highly accurate and no blood had come back positive in over a month – the members of the task force had been authorized to speak publicly about it.

****

"So you two are who America has to thank for putting a stop to a terrifying disease," the television personality began, crossing one slender leg over another and leaning forward in her seat. The pretty African-American woman often found herself being compared to Oprah, which Julianne Jackson didn't mind in the least. It was a sign of respect for her and her show that people would mention her in the same vain as arguably the most successful daytime talk show host ever.

"Well, not exactly," Isaac replied, shifting a bit in his chair as he tried to get more comfortable. *Little chance of that since they dressed me up in a suit and a tie that feels more like a noose*, he thought. "I hate ties," Isaac had complained to the fashion designer who presented him with his selected outfit for the interview. "I'm sorry, Dr. Carlson," the woman had replied in a surprisingly sympathetic tone, "but you really should wear a suit and tie. You'll look unprofessional if you don't." Isaac reluctantly agreed, and now here he was thinking he would've rather walked out wearing Keri's green shift dress, since at least the V-neck on it allowed her to breathe.

Realizing that Keri, Julianne, and the audience were all waiting for him to continue speaking, Isaac brought his thoughts back to the present. "To begin with, a point of medical clarification, it wasn't a disease. We were dealing with a virus. And Keri and I," he added, gesturing to his deputy as he spoke, "were only two of the members of the task force."

"That's right," the onetime reporter said as she referenced the notes in her lap. "There were six of you in all, correct?"

"Correct," answered Keri. "Isaac and myself, plus Lean Mann, Anthony Russo, Gill Pingrey, and of course David Malhotra."

"Right. I want to get to Dr. Malhotra's story later. So sad. But first, for the members of our audience either here or at home who might not know, why don't you explain a little bit of how this task force came about and what it is your assignment was."

"Okay," Isaac replied, nodding his head. "Well, first, I'll give you a little bit of background."

Keri couldn't help but smile as her boss, per his usual, ignored whatever question was actually asked and talked about what he wanted to.

"Keri and I work at the National Institutes of Health in Bethesda, Maryland. It's a medical research facility and an agency of the Department of Health and Human Services."

The interviewer patiently nodded her head in understanding, recognizing that it was going to be a challenge to get this Dr. Carlson character to simply answer the questions he was asked. Normally that kind of thing drove Julianne crazy, but this was a highly coveted interview and guaranteed to boost her ratings. So she just sat there, and nodded, and waited.

"Drs. Malhotra and Pingrey are with the Centers for Disease Control in Atlanta," Isaac continued, "and Drs. Mann and Russo mostly do contract work for the government out of their lab at Hopkins."

"Johns Hopkins?" Julianne asked to clarify.

"Yes, Johns Hopkins. In Baltimore."

The talk show host then turned her attention to Keri. "Dr. Dupree, let's bring you in to the conversation a bit. So you have this task force, this *virus*," she emphasized, smiling at Isaac, "and this group of patients. What was it like? Is this a standing group that works together or were you all pulled together specifically for this?"

"Specifically for this," replied Keri. Julianne liked this woman already – she answered the question she was asked.

"The medical community as a whole is very large," Keri continued, "but the infectious disease field is pretty small. We generally all know each other or at least know of each other from medical school or conferences or things like that, and word tends to spread quickly if there's a new virus or illness popping up anywhere."

Keri hesitated, half-expecting Isaac to jump in and take over. When he didn't, she kept talking. "Reports started coming in to the NIH and CDC about patients dying of a mysterious illness. It was loosely termed 'SuperAIDS' because it had the same symptoms as AIDS but was killing people much, much faster."

"One month as opposed to ten years," the interviewer chimed in.

Isaac and Keri both nodded their heads grimly. "Yes," Isaac verified.

"Okay, so then what?" Julianne pressed. "You start getting reports about this crazy new illness . . ."

This time Isaac did answer the question. "At the same time that we were first hearing about these patients, the White House was as well. President Hughes and his staff kept a fairly open line of communication between the West Wing and the Director of the CDC, and when Director Clark told the White House about the mysterious deaths and their increasing number, President Hughes decided to put together a team of doctors and researchers to figure out what was going on."

"And you were named the head of this task force?" asked Julianne.

"I was," Isaac answered with only the slightest twinge of arrogance in his voice. *He's really trying hard to make a good impression*, Keri thought.

The seasoned TV personality noticed the red light blinking just above Camera One and knew that it was her cue. "Unfortunately we have to take a quick break, but don't go anywhere because we will be back soon with more from the SuperAIDS doctors."

FORTY-NINE

From somewhere in a corner a man's voice yelled "and we're clear," at which point Julianne released a deep sigh and raised her arms above her head to stretch. She loved doing in-depth, hot topic interviews like this one, but having to maintain perfect posture and pose the whole time always made her back stiff.

"I'm sorry," Keri began, "but do I have time to run to the restroom really quickly?"

"Make it fast," answered a producer who had appeared seemingly out of nowhere to hand the show's host a new flashcard with a fresh set of notes on it.

As Keri stood up and began her mad dash to the nearest bathroom, Julianne noticed that her other guest still looked a bit nervous. "Don't worry," she smiled reassuringly. "You're doing great."

"You really think so?" Isaac was noticeably uneasy, with his desire to make a good impression aggravated by the fact that he was hardly ever nervous about anything and therefore didn't really know how to handle the butterflies still flying around at warp speed in his stomach.

Julianne smiled again. "I really think so."

"Back in ten!" the same male voice yelled, and both the host and her guest momentarily panicked when they realized that Keri hadn't returned from the bathroom yet.

"Just zoom in on me until she gets back," Julianne told the man operating the large camera in the center of the soundstage.

"Three, two, one –"

Once again the interviewer's back was ramrod straight as the show went live on the air. The smile she had given Isaac was also gone, replaced by a very serious, Edward R. Murrow-esque face.

"Welcome back to the show," Julianne began, deliberately avoiding cutting her eyes to the side as Keri quietly but quickly crept back in to her seat beside Isaac. "We're here today with Drs. Isaac Carlson and Keri Dupree, two members of the task force that tackled the deadly virus responsible for killing twenty-seven Americans."

Pivoting in her chair as the camera panned wide to include the show's two guests, Julianne said: "Dr. Carlson, back to you. How did you do it? You've got this deadly virus – how did you fight it and eventually beat it?"

Isaac had been in the medical profession long enough to know when he could go into a lot of scientific detail and when he couldn't. This audience, the live one in front of him and the millions more watching from home, were definitely not prepared to take a crash course in genome sequencing, serum testing, and the multitude of other things that Isaac would have to talk about to truly explain the work of the task force. So, just as he had done with FBI agent Reagan White several months earlier, Dr. Carlson translated things into English. And everyone in the room marveled at the information as if they were listening to Albert Einstein.

"Wow. You know," Julianne said with a smile, "I was never one to really like science in school. But all of the things that your group did were truly fascinating."

Both Isaac and Keri beamed with pride at the woman's compliment.

"Now, we really can't talk about the task force and the great work you all did without mentioning David Malhotra's story," the interviewer said. "Dr. Dupree, maybe you could share a little bit of that with us?"

Keri didn't want to talk about David's story. It was too sad. Too heartbreaking. Too much of a cruel twist of fate. Keri took a deep breath and slowly released it since she knew that David's was a story that deserved to be told. At least part of it.

Keri opened her mouth to speak, but at first the words wouldn't come out. All she could think about was the way David's eyes had lit up every time someone mentioned his twins. The way he talked about them every chance he got, showed their pictures to everyone willing to look, and called them without fail every afternoon at 3:45pm to ask how their day at school had been. A tear slowly rolled down Keri's cheek as she thought for the thousandth time that her colleague was the kind of father that she hoped her husband Scott would be one day.

"It's okay," Julianne said gently, reaching over to hand Keri a tissue. "Take your time."

Keri wiped away the few other tears that had escaped and began to speak. Addressing the audience instead of her interviewer, she said:

"Dr. Malhotra, David, works for a special unit of the CDC that deals specifically with infectious diseases and other pathogens like the one we were working against. The task force was working out of the NIH headquarters near DC," Keri explained, "so David had rented a hotel room and would stay up there during the week. If it was at all possible, he flew home to Atlanta on the weekends."

You could have heard a pin drop when Keri paused to take a breath, with everyone in the room waiting to hear what happened next.

"David is married," Keri continued, "and has – had – two twins . . . a boy and a girl." Keri tried to ignore the gasps she heard from audience members as some of them guessed what was coming. "The twins were in a car accident and were injured pretty badly." Keri was careful not to go into too much detail – the gist of the story had already been reported on the news, but she didn't want to invade the Malhotras' privacy any further by giving out new details on national television.

"Both of the children required blood transfusions, which, as Isaac explained earlier, were how the virus was being transmitted." Dr. Dupree found herself having to pause again to close her eyes and take a deep breath. Every word she spoke just reminded her more of the anguish she had seen on the faces of David and his family in the news footage of when they buried little Matthew.

A comforting hand on the side of her arm caused Keri to open her eyes in surprise. It was Isaac, with the same sadness she was feeling displayed clearly on his face. "It's okay," he said quietly. "I can finish it."

Isaac didn't want to talk about Matty Malhotra either, but he would. People should know the kind of sacrifice David had made. Sitting up straight and blinking the moisture from his eyes, Isaac took over.

"Jane, David's daughter, made a complete recovery. Unfortunately, very sadly, the transfusion that David's son received was tainted with the virus." Isaac lowered his head and his voice before adding: "Matty didn't make it."

The audience members who hadn't caught on while Keri was talking now issued their own gasps of shock and sadness. Seeing that time was running out for the show, Julianne pushed forward. "But Dr. Malhotra didn't quit the task force, did he?"

"No," Keri confirmed. "He didn't. He worked from Atlanta and would use Skype or FaceTime when he needed to talk to the group."

Isaac nodded. "He said that figuring out a way to stop the virus was the best thing he could do to honor his son's memory."

"Incredible," the talk show host said, shaking her head in amazement. Then, noticing the blinking red light yet again, she added: "I'm afraid we're going to have to end there since our time is up. But I do want to say, just for anyone watching, that there haven't been any new cases of this virus in over a month and the government considers it to no longer be a risk to the public."

"That's correct," Isaac confirmed.

"Well, thank you so much for being on the show today and for all of your hard work." Turning to face the center camera, Julianne concluded: "and thank you for watching. Be sure to tune in tomorrow to see circus animals performing right here on this stage."

****

"All good things must come to an end, I guess."

There was a certain amount of sadness in Joseph's voice as he spoke, his comment in reaction to the recorded interview he was watching on television. Joseph had been busy when the show initially aired, and he definitely wanted to watch the special 'Outbreak: Tainted Blood' from the comfort of his own couch. *Mere steps away from where said blood was tainted*, Joseph thought gleefully.

"And it worked!" he exclaimed, suddenly jumping off the couch and onto his feet. "It worked it worked it worked it worked!" Joseph's hands clapped in unison with his chant as he bounced up and down like a schoolgirl. "It really, really worked!"

The evil genius behind the outbreak wasn't exaggerating, either. The virus' impact on humans went well beyond anything he had observed in the mice or cats, and the number of deaths from the mysterious illness – combined with its completely random selection of victims – had left all of America terrified to go to the hospital. In reaction to the very public freak-out, Joseph's office had been flooded with phone calls and emails asking him to serve on new infectious disease boards, teach pathology courses at prestigious universities, and basically everything else that he had ever wanted as far as recognition and respect were concerned. The people of the United States now understood all too well how important pathology was and just how rare medical researchers of Joseph's caliber were.

"It worked," he said once again, this time at a whisper. "And I got away with it." There was no more need to yell. Joseph was content. For the first time in his life, he was really, truly content.

FIFTY

"So how does it feel to be back working normal cases?" Lois asked. Dr. Carlson had always been a workaholic, but the viral outbreak had taken things to a completely new level and the friendly NIH receptionist sometimes felt like she saw Isaac more often than she saw her own husband. Especially since the now-famous doctor liked to pace the halls while he was thinking, with his favored path crossing in front of her desk several times.

"None of my cases are normal, Lois," Isaac replied. The receptionist used to think it was arrogance, but after solving such an incredibly complicated medical mystery, Lois now believed that Isaac had every right to be as confident as he was. It's not bragging if it's true.

Lois smiled. "Right. Of course, Dr. Carlson." Switching topics, she added: "how is Dr. Dupree doing, by the way?"

"She's fine, I guess," Isaac grimaced in reply. Shortly after their interview aired on television, Keri had announced that she was expecting her first baby. Scott, Keri's husband, was absolutely thrilled, and everyone could tell that Keri was excited about it as well. After having been a part of such a groundbreaking, exhausting, and thrilling task force, Dr. Dupree had decided it was finally time to cave on the baby issue. She had also come to realize just how precious life was, and Scott had already agreed that if the baby was a boy they would call him Matty.

Sensing that Lois was expecting more of a response than 'she's fine,' Isaac continued: "she tells me different stuff about how big it is now and all of that, but to be honest I don't pay that much attention. Next time she wants to talk babies I'll just send her down here to you."

Lois beamed and nodded her head in reply, stereotypically overjoyed to 'ooh' and 'ahh' and giggle over her coworker's pregnancy.

Isaac rolled his eyes and turned to walk toward the door to leave for the day when the chatty woman stopped him. "Oh, wait, I almost forgot. A box arrived for you just a few minutes ago. The delivery man said it wasn't time sensitive so I figured I'd just wait to give it to you when you left for the day. Which is now." Lois smiled again. She liked Dr. Carlson – in her book, he was definitely one of the good guys.

The doctor offered a slight grin in response, the bags under his eyes betraying just how hard he had been working the past several months and how much it had taken out of him. Isaac put his briefcase down on the floor beside the reception desk and picked the card off the top of the box. Grief replaced the smile that had briefly graced Isaac's face as he read the note inside the envelope.

"It's another thank you from a patient's family. This one's from the parents of Bobby Hill." Isaac sighed as the details of the boy's illness rushed back into his mind. He remembered them all. "Bobby Hill. Eleven years old from North Carolina. Originally treated for injuries sustained in a four-wheeler accident. Died three weeks after his transfusion."

Lois was amazed by Dr. Carlson's ability to remember so many details about so many patients.

"The Hills are just like the others have been," Isaac added, holding up the card in his hand to reference it. "Thanking me for giving them closure by finding out how their boy died." The pathologist shook his head. "I'll never understand why they still thank me even after he's dead."

The longtime receptionist on the other side of the desk from Isaac knew that his last words weren't meant to elicit a response, so she let it go without comment. She couldn't even imagine the amount of stress that the doctors on the outbreak task force had been under – especially Isaac as the head of the team – and her seventeen years as a receptionist and twenty-five years as a wife and mother taught her that sometimes people just want someone who will listen. Lois could see that this had been one of those moments for Dr. Carlson.

Isaac shook his head to clear out the cobwebs. "Anyway, enough of that. I'm headed home to try to catch up on some sleep. Have a good night."

"You too," Lois replied.

****

Isaac had just reached his car in the employee parking lot when he heard someone call his name.

"Dr. Carlson, wait!"

Isaac set the Hills' gift box on top of his car and turned to see the NIH receptionist, Lois, doing her best to jog toward him in heels and a pencil skirt. It would have been quite comical, actually, if he hadn't been able to see how much difficulty the woman was having.

Lois was breathing heavily as she finally reached Isaac's car. "You forgot your briefcase," she said in between breaths.

"Oh, wow, yes I did. Thank you so much," Isaac said gratefully as he took the leather bag that Lois was handing him. "Although I wouldn't have been able to get very far without it . . . my keys are in here." Isaac pulled his car keys from a side pocket of the briefcase. "I'm sorry to make you run all the way out here."

"Oh, it's not a problem," the woman replied with yet another smile, having now caught her breath. "I could use the exercise."

Isaac issued a courtesy laugh in response as he pushed a button to unlock the doors and then moved the gift box from his car's roof to its backseat. The doctor thought his conversation with the overly friendly receptionist was finished, so he said a quick "see you tomorrow" before turning to open the driver's door.

"Yep!" came the woman's chipper reply. And then: "I never knew Isaac wasn't your real name."

Dr. Carlson stopped in his tracks, one foot already inside the car and one still on the pavement. "I'm sorry, what?"

"The tag on your briefcase," Lois explained. "It says that Isaac is your middle name."

"Oh, yeah. Isaac's not my first name, but it's still my *real* name," he answered with irritation. It bothered him when people said that the name he had always gone by professionally wasn't his 'real' name.

Lois was able to squeeze in one more question as Isaac lowered himself into his car. "So what's the J in 'J. Isaac' stand for?"

"Joseph," he answered, and shut the door.

###

VICTIM APPENDIX

Tre'shon Abner   Los Angeles, CA 19
  gunshot wound

Ashley Crabb   Germantown, TN 16
  car accident

Linzy Crabb   Germantown, TN 13
  car accident

Thomas George   Lubbock, TX   48
  MRSA

Andrew Gray   San Francisco, CA 30
  assault & battery

Mitch Hanson   Louisville, KY   52
  heart attack

Elena Hernandez   Rye, NY   34
  miscarriage

Bobby Hill   Charlotte, NC   11
  four-wheeler accident

Edna Jenkins   Denver, CO   83
  car accident

Marcus Johnson   Knoxville, TN   21
  knee surgery

Maryanne Jones   Las Vegas, NV   86
  hip surgery

Alicia Kendrick   Philadelphia, PA 33
  grease fire burns

Jane Lambert   Greenville, SC   64
  colon cancer

Teresa Lewis   Huntsville, AL   28
  parasite

Matthew Malhotra Atlanta, GA   12
  car accident

John Martinez   Columbus, OH   56
  lung transplant

Lisa Masters	Phoenix, AZ	40
breast cancer		
Chuck McKenna	Providence, OK	43
hunting accident		
Diane Parker	Boston, MA	50
throat cancer		
Cooper Simanski	Long Island, NY	8 days
premature birth		
Juan Sosa	Miami, FL	39
stomach cancer		
Holly Steinberger	Akron, OH	62
liver cirrhosis		
Taylor Stone	Houston, TX	17
leukemia		
Dakota Thompson	Cheyenne, WY	9
brain tumor		
Julius Wilkes	Atlanta, GA	15
gunshot wound		
Nick Williams	Orlando, FL	70
prostate cancer		
Peter Young	Jackson, MS	34
gastric bypass surgery		

ABOUT THE AUTHOR

Danielle knew she was born to be a writer at age four when she entertained an entire emergency room with the - false - story of how she was adopted. *Do No Harm* is Danielle's second novel. She is a graduate of Georgetown University (Go Hoyas!) and Harvard Law School. Danielle lives in Georgia with her chocolate lab, Gus.